Poppy's Moth

by Timothy Noakes

with a foreword and afterword
by Poppy Grove

Published 2024

All rights reserved

Copyright © Lopinga Books

Cover illustrations: Wikipedia Commons

The moral right of the author has been asserted

ISBN 978-19164631-1-0

Lopinga Books www.lopinga.com

A Foreword from Poppy

I was eleven when I met Moth and this story is what happened to us from then until, some five years later, I had our baby. I won't tell you anything much about what happened in between, it would spoil the story.

When we met we lived in England and spoke English, although Moth also knew some French. By the time we started to write what became this book we lived in France but still spoke English to each other when we weren't with French friends. The first bit of the book we wrote in English but the second half of our story (the really exciting bit) we recorded while talking to each other about our adventures. We spoke in an ancient language that has never been written down. You'll find out how we learnt it as you read our book.

By the time we were ready to turn our private story into a book that might be published, we were seventeen. It was difficult, but fun, to try and remember how we felt and thought when we were eleven or twelve. Maybe we have made our young selves seem more grown-up than we really were.

Moth and I lived this story and wrote it together but it seemed to work best if just one of us told it.

That's why Moth is named as the author and I got part of the title. Now it's time to read our story: I hope you enjoy it.

Poppy Grove, Ariège, France

CONTENTS

Chapter 1 – The Sleep-out

I'd never seen Poppy before. The other six kids I'd known for years, ever since we were five and had started school in the next village. We were going to have a sleep-out at our village nature reserve and had been getting ready for it since yesterday.

My Dad came over with this girl I'd never seen before and said 'This is Poppy, she's just moved to our village – in the house where Ruth used to live. I knew Poppy's Mum years ago and she's asked me to help Poppy make some friends before she starts at school next week. She'll be in year seven like you so there's a good chance she'll be in your class because there's a space now Ruth has moved away.'

Before I could reply, Dad continued 'Everything and everyone will be a bit strange for Poppy. Will you look after her at the sleep-out and let her meet all your friends?'

'Of course I will Dad. Come on Poppy, let's go and find out what we have to do first.'

Elspeth's Mum, one of the parents who had organised the sleep-out, said 'Listen everyone, we want this to be fun and without lots of rules. But remember, this is a nature reserve and we mustn't disturb the wildlife or upset the sheep and their lambs. Oh, and there's no toilet, so if you want a wee it's a wild-wee, just go behind a tree or a bush. If you need a poo then take one of these trowels with you, dig a little pit and bury everything after you. Then go to the bowser to wash your hands.'

"Bowser" is a funny name, it's a tank on wheels that you can hitch to a car and fill with water. The water is meant for the sheep to drink but they can spare a bit if we need to wash our hands.

'OK, the first task is to split yourself into two groups, one will get the bonfire going and help make the bread for lunch, while the others can make your straw house for tonight. Who wants to make the house?'

I saw Poppy put up her hand so I did too, even though the bonfire sounded more fun.

The sheep had eaten almost all the hay that was stored in the barn for their winter feed but beside the barn was a haystack made of bales that were no good for the sheep. They had too much ragwort in the hay and ragwort is poisonous to sheep. So we were going to make our house with straw bales borrowed from a farmer and some of the poisonous hay – it's a good job we are not sheep.

Just as I was going to help Poppy start carrying the hay bales to the campsite, Jacob ran by:

'Come-on Moth, I'm going for a wild-wee, I bet I can get higher up the tree than you can.'

So I had to go, well I needed to really. Jacob won by a full six inches and I said it was because he had needed to go more than I did. He disagreed and said it was because his was longer than mine.

As I was doing up my zip he said 'I bet girls wish they had willies, it can't be much fun crouching in the stinging nettles. Whose your new girlfriend by-the-way?' 'She's not my girlfriend, she's just moved here and my Dad wants her to meet us all before school starts again. She's called Poppy.'

Dominic and Elspeth had carried a few straw bales to the campsite while I'd been away. Then Poppy reappeared from somewhere and we all got some more bales. The others were preparing to light the bonfire. It wasn't too hard to build the straw hut. We decided that we would all sleep in line so the floor-space of the hut had to be as wide as the tallest of us and as long as eight of us side by side in our sleeping bags. Then Dominic pointed out that we should make it wider than that, in case someone needed to get out at night. He was right of course, so that was what we did. We had used nearly all the bales by the time we had made the walls of the hut three bales high. It wasn't going to be a very tall hut, we'd just have to stoop to go in and out.

We made the roof with poles that had been cut in the wood, they reached across the width of the hut roof and then we put a tarpaulin on and stretched it as tight as we could. That should be waterproof but we used the rest of the hay to go on top of the tarpaulin and held it down with more poles. That looked much more natural. Now it was time to test it.

Elspeth said 'We've made it, so I think we should have first choice about where our sleeping bags go. The others can choose later.'

Poppy said 'Can I be next to Moth, because I know him a bit and to Elspeth because she's a girl?'

I went right to the far end of the hut with Poppy on the other side and Elspeth beyond Poppy. Dominic wasn't certain what he wanted to do and said he'd choose when the others came.

We went to see the bread-makers. The bread dough had been kneaded and pummelled into two big lumps that were sitting on metal dishes near the fire.

Someone said 'Let's make bread rolls then we won't have to cut the loaves into slices.'

So we made lots of little balls of dough and arranged them a bit apart on the metal dishes. Elspeth's Mum said the rolls would need to rise until they were twice as fat as they were now and that would take at least half an hour. We should go for an explore and come back then.

'Come-on Poppy, let's go and see the sheep and their lambs.' 'Yes please – but why does everyone call you Moth?'

'I'll tell you while we watch the sheep.'

So we crossed the field and sat by the fence watching the mother sheep grazing, while their lambs kept butting them in the udder and wagging their tails madly as they got a quick drink of their mum's milk. I explained to Poppy that my real name is Timothy and Moth is kind of short for that but the real reason is that I'm interested in moths and like keeping caterpillars until they hatch as butterflies or moths.

'You can see some moths tonight, Poppy, because Peter is bringing his moth trap so we can see the ones he catches.'

'Who is he and does the trap kill all the poor moths?'

'He's an old man and I've known him for years. Peter knows lots about moths, he's written books about them and it was because of him that I got interested. He gave me caterpillars to keep even before I started school. The moth trap is a bright light that attracts the moths and there's a box under the light where they hide, it doesn't hurt them and you let them go once you know what they are and have photographed them if you want to.'

Poppy didn't reply for a while, she seemed to be counting sheep.

'Moth, there are seven mother sheep and thirteen lambs. Do sheep always have twins? Has one of the lambs died or run away?'

'No – four of the ewes had twins but one had triplets and two only had one lamb each. Look, that's the littlest triplet. He doesn't get enough milk from his mother, so someone comes and gives him milk in a bottle twice a day.'

'I'd love to feed a lamb, do you think I could?'

'Yes, I'll ask Mrs Howberry.'

'Do you know everyone in the village, Moth?' 'Almost: I've lived here all my life and it's a small village but I know the families of my school friends best. I'll soon know you and your family too I hope.'

Poppy went back to thinking about sheep 'Where's the father sheep? Ram, I mean. Do you keep him somewhere else?'

'He lives in the next village and belongs to a family who have some sheep of their own. Last autumn we sent our ewes to stay with the ram, they came back here pregnant and had their lambs about three weeks ago.'

'My Mum's pregnant.'

'Do you want a little sister?'

'What I'm getting is twin brothers. They should arrive in six weeks or so.'

'Can I come and feed them if they have bottles?'
'Mum wants to feed them herself I think. They won't be able to wag their tails while she does though.'

'Those rolls should be ready to cook. Let's go and feed ourselves.'

The rolls were ready, they had grown so they touched their neighbours and each tray in turn was fitted in a big tin and rested on the embers of the bonfire to cook. The smell of the wood-smoke and the cooking rolls was lovely and so was the bread when it was cooked. The cooking team hadn't just made the bread rolls, they had collected a sack full of young stinging nettle shoots and were boiling them in a cauldron hanging from a metal tripod over the fire. There was also a big frying pan of sausages and mushrooms. The mushrooms said Tesco on the bag, so they weren't proper wild ones but they still tasted good. So did the nettles, they went into a dark green mess like spinach does when it's cooked but I thought they tasted much nicer than spinach.

When everyone had finished their meal and cleared things away, Elspeth's Mum got the others to organise their sleeping bag positions, it was already past four o'clock. Most of us wandered off for a wild wee. Mrs Howberry arrived and I asked her if Poppy could feed "little triplet". His milk is special lamb's milk powder that you dissolve in water and put in an old beer bottle with a big rubber feeding teat on it.

At first the lamb would not come close to Poppy.

'Let some milk spill out of the teat so he sees it and smells it.'

Then he started feeding, slurping the milk and wagging his tail like the other lambs did when feeding from their mothers. He nearly emptied the beer bottle before he had drunk enough.

'That's enough, let's leave the sheep now. You need to be a bit careful where you put your feet in this field Poppy.'

'Yes, why can't they train the sheep to use little trowels like they did us?'

Peter had set up his moth trap right on the far side of the field. It had a little generator to make the electricity; you could only just hear the purr of the motor when you were in our hut. They said we should all get ready for bed, even though it was still quite early. It would soon be dark and, in the middle of the night, we would be getting up to see what moths had been caught and then we could explore the reserve at midnight.

Getting to sleep at seven o'clock is never easy, especially in a straw hut with a bunch of your friends on a sort of adventure. We'd had a quick face-wipe and tooth-wash at the bowser and then, back in the hut, taken off a few clothes and slipped into sleeping-bags. I turned on my side and faced the straw wall at the end of the hut, so Poppy could get into her bag without me staring at her. I don't think I need have worried; I saw later that she had kept her pants and vest on, then pyjamas and finally a pullover, just like the rest of us. It's quite cold in April.

I couldn't get to sleep. Do sheep baa all night? How many moths would there be – April's too early for the best ones. What about Poppy? Can you have a friend who is a girl – or is that the same as a girlfriend? I turned over and Poppy looked as though she was asleep but she opened her eyes, looked at me and smiled. I didn't know what to do, so I said 'baa' like one of the sheep just had. She laughed, smiled and said:

'Thank you Moth for a lovely day, I think I shall enjoy living here.'

Then she kissed me. I didn't know if I should return her kiss. I turned over again, listened to the sheep and thought I'd better count the baas. I woke up when Dominic's Dad stuck his head in the hut and said it was time to look at the moths.

Spring is not the best time for moths. In the summer holidays you get big hawk-moths and lovely shiny ones called burnished brasses and hundreds of others. But I'd never been up in the middle of the night to see moths, normally I just went in the morning, with Peter, to help sort out the ones that had been caught the previous night.

The trap was still on and we'd been warned not to stare at the light because it might damage our eyes. There was a big white sheet under the trap and some moths had settled on the sheet instead of going into the trap. Peter gave us some butterfly nets and little cardboard boxes with clear plastic lids. We had to catch one of each kind of moth, box them and then try to find out what they were called using Peter's books. I caught one of the bigger ones that had a nice dark, mottled, camouflage sort of pattern on its wings.

I thought I knew what it was 'Is this a Brindled Beauty, Peter?'

'Yes, that's right, well done.'

'How did you know that one?' asked Poppy.

'I bred some once, the caterpillars look just like sticks but have yellow rings round their bodies when they are young.'

'What's this little one, it's like a grey arrowhead?'

'That's another one I know: it's a male March Moth.'

'It's April now so it's a bit late then, isn't it? How do you know it's a male – I can't see its willy?'

'Because it's got wings. The females look like spiders but with only six legs. They crawl up trees and wait for a male to find them.'

'Glad I'm not a March Moth then.'

We'd sorted out about ten different kinds of moth, which is quite good for April, but Poppy didn't seem as interested in them as I was. 'What do you like doing Poppy?' This was a dangerous question, she might say ballet dancing or playing the violin. Her reply was a relief 'Star-watching.' 'Come on then, it's just the time to see some and you can tell me what they are.'

Near the moth trap the light meant you couldn't see any stars. Even further away from it, the lights from the town where we went to school made it difficult. 'Look, Poppy, if we go down into the scrub area, where the wide paths go through the bushes, it should be good for star-watching. The bushes block out the light and you can look up at a dark part of the sky.'

'Let's lie down on the grass here, it makes it easier to look up. I wish I'd brought my binoculars with me.'

Poppy went on 'It's a good job there's no moon yet tonight, we can see the stars quite well. See that really bright one up there? It's a planet not a star. I think it's Jupiter but it might be Venus; I need my book that tells you where each planet is at this time of year to be certain.'

'There must be thousands of stars – have they all got names?' 'I think there's millions and most of them have just got numbers. The names I like best are the ones that have been used for thousands of years. In the olden days people sat and watched the stars because there wasn't any telly. They saw patterns in the stars that looked like animals or people and gave names to each group of stars. Then they made up stories about what these star animals and people did. Twelve of those names are still used for birthday star signs. I'll be twelve on the 12th of August so I'm a Leo.'

'I was twelve on 14th of February.' 'That's Aquarius and Valentine's day too, I'll have to remember to send you a card.'

'Can you see Leo or Aquarius now?' 'No, I can't see any of the birthday star signs but look over there, quite low down, can you see four bright stars that are nearly a square and with a curved tail of stars joined on at the top? It looks a bit like a saucepan and it's a constellation with one of the old names' 'Yes, is "Saucepan" what they called it?' 'No, the ancients called it the Great Bear – odd because bears don't have tails.'

Then she showed me Orion, a hunter whose belt was made of three stars that are easy to see and a little group of dimmer stars that make up his huntsman's dagger. One of the stars in his head is called Beetle Juice (at least that is what it sounded like). Poppy said 'It's a red giant and will soon blow up.' 'How soon?' 'They say anytime in the next few thousand years.' 'Oh, I shall look forward to it.'

Then we just lay beside each other, staring up at the stars and thinking our own thoughts. 'Poppy, do you think God made all these stars?' She paused a little then said 'Didn't you know, they were made by Father Christmas and the Tooth Fairy?' 'I haven't believed in them for years.' 'Me neither.'

'OK, so what do your star scientists say happened?'

'That's the trouble, the astronomers keep changing their minds. There was supposed to have been a big bang that created all the stars and before that happened there was nothing at all, not even anywhere for nothing to be part of. It can't have been a big bang because sound only goes through something real, not through space, so it was probably just a big flash. Some people say there are lots of universes and you can't get from one to another. Others say there was something before the big bang but they don't know what. It's very confusing. There used to be a famous scientist who lived near here, in Cambridge, (not the one in the wheel chair). He said the universe had always existed and always would, when old stars blew-up or died new ones formed to replace them. Now he's dead, everyone says he was wrong but I hope he turns out to have been right.'

By now it was well past midnight, time to go home to bed in the straw-hut.

'Back in a minute' she said, and went off into the bushes. I went the other way and did the same. We had to creep past all the others who had come back from the moth-trapping earlier, they were asleep already. We crawled into our sleeping bags and looked at each other.

Poppy leaned across and said 'Thank you Moth for a lovely night too' and kissed me again.

'Poppy, can I ask you something? Jacob said something and it's been puzzling me all day.'

'Go on then.'

'Do girls wish they had willies?'

I could see she was nearly laughing and wished I hadn't asked. Eventually she turned the nearly-laugh into a smile and said 'When I've had a good look at yours, I'll tell you if I'm jealous.'

Not quite the answer I'd expected but I think Poppy is going to be fun.

Chapter 2 – Planting a Tree with Poppy

It was only a day until we started school again. Poppy would be going on the bus with the rest of us and was going to be in my class. I wanted to see her house, although I already knew what it was like from when Ruth had lived there. I thought Poppy wouldn't mind if I called to tell her where the buses stopped and why there are three school buses for our village when there are only about ten of us who get the bus each day.

She was in the garden reading a book. 'Hello Poppy, what's the book about?'

'Romans and how they were nearly chased out of our part of England by Queen Boudicca.'

'I thought you liked stars, not history.'

'I like both and they get mixed up when you want to know about the astrologers who lived hundreds or thousands of years ago.'

'There's a Roman road near here, let's go on a walk along part of it.'

'Yes, that sounds fun. I've seen the road on the map, I'll go and get it.'

'Mum, can we go for a walk along the Roman road?'

'Yes love, as long as it's not too busy and you get back for lunch.'

'Oh Mum, don't be silly, it's a footpath these days not a main road and I've got my phone if there are any problems.'

I thought Poppy's Mum looked ill. Of course she was fat with the twins inside her waiting to be born.

She was probably just tired and a bit worried. We waved goodbye and went.

'The first bit of the road that's marked on the map is near the nature reserve; let's go and start there then follow the path back this way.'

It only took ten minutes going round the edge of some fields to get to the Roman road path. This part was a farm track, wide enough for tractors to use, and so it was easy to follow.

After a while I said 'I bet there must be loads of Roman coins near this path. We should borrow one of those metal detectors and see what we find. Some people with detectors came to the nature reserve last year and found a Roman coin: they gave it to us because it wasn't a rare one.'

Poppy said 'I wonder how it got there? Surely the Roman would have stayed on the road, not gone off through the woods, unless there was a little farm or something over there.'

'Probably he went off for a wild wee and lost the coin when he lifted his toga.'

'More likely he was hiding in the undergrowth because Boudicca's army was after him. When they found him, they stripped him bare and he lost his life as well as his penny.'

I wondered if she is really good at history or just at making up good stories. Presently the farm track turned into a path through a strip of woodland. As we got into the shade of the trees we could see straight on through the whole length of the wood.

Poppy said 'Roman roads are always straight' and was just going to add something else when a fox appeared, almost as far away as we could see, but he was coming towards us.

I whispered to Poppy 'Stay still, the wind is blowing from him to us so he might not smell us.'

He kept on coming and when he was quite close he stopped near a tussock of grass, watched for a bit and then jumped and pounced down on the tussock. When he looked up he had a vole in his jaws. He looked round, suddenly saw us, and disappeared into the bushes leaving a strong smell behind him. The smell was neither nasty nor nice, just foxy, but also somehow a bit exciting. I tried to explain that to Poppy and she said she thought she knew what I meant.

Poppy said 'She must have been a vixen catching some food for her cubs.'

I thought the dog foxes fed their cubs too but I wasn't quite sure.

There was no point trying to follow the fox, so we tried to follow the way he or she had come.

'Look at this Poppy.'

'It's dog poo – revolting!'

'I'm not a poo expert but I know enough to be sure this is fox poo. You can smell the fox and if you look close you can see what it has been eating – lots of black beetles.'

She had a quick look and a sniff and agreed there was no doubt.

I don't think Poppy was as excited by the fox poo as I was.

'I don't want to eat beetles or voles, can we go back to Mum's for lunch?'

Her Mum still looked a bit tired and ill. Poppy had said it would be a few weeks before the babies are due but I bet her Mum wishes it were sooner. After lunch I checked with Poppy that she knew where to wait for the bus tomorrow and then I went home to finish the project I should have done at the start of the holiday.

Next day, Poppy was at the stop before me. Even though the buses come through half-a-dozen villages and are nearly full before they get to us (we're the last village before the school) you can nearly always find a double seat and sit with a friend. That's because everyone else does the same – it's a very odd person who sits on their own. So Poppy and I shared a seat and arrived for her first day at our school.

I'm not going to say much about school, it's a world of its own, even your friends don't seem the same as when you are playing at home. Poppy wasn't always in the same classes that I went to but mostly she was. She's really good at Maths and History, but not as good as I am at French, so we got in the habit of meeting after school to help each other with homework.

Everyone thinks I'm good at French because Dad is a French teacher but in a different school from mine. I'm glad he's not at our school, it would be horridly embarrassing trying not to notice when your mates said something nasty or rude about your Dad, like they do about all the teachers however good they are. Dad's a good teacher but he didn't teach me French, just made sure I learnt it naturally.

When I was five Mum and Dad bought a cottage right down in the southern part of France and we've spent our summer holidays there ever since. There aren't many people who live in our French village but there is a family from Toulouse who come to their holiday cottage most weekends and holidays. Philippe is about the same age as me and his sister Emilie about two years older. We soon started playing together but even though they didn't know any English it seemed quite easy to understand the games they played and to join in. Soon I could understand what their Mum and Dad said too.

Obviously I learned slowly at first, just separate words and little phrases. If you think about it, that's how everybody learns to speak their own language. A baby only has to say 'cat' or 'ball' or 'milk' or 'dummy' and you know he means 'look at that cat' 'throw me the ball' 'I want some milk' or 'I'm not happy and want a cuddle.' One word is as good as a sentence at that age and when, a bit older, he says 'I swimmed yesterday' nobody is unkind enough to tell him he's got it wrong. He just learns when to say 'swam' without being told or thinking about it.

When I was nine, Dad got a job teaching English at a French school for a year, so we lived in our holiday house and I went to a local school where all the teaching was in French. I learnt as much in the playground as I did in the classroom and by the time we came back to England I could speak French pretty well. I wasn't so good at writing it though.

I'd told all this to Poppy then asked why she was good at Maths and History.

'I don't know about Maths, I've just always liked doing number puzzles and thinking about really big numbers, like how far it is to the nearest star. Some people are scared of numbers but if you're not, they can be fun and fairly easy. History is different and we've got lots of history books because Mum used to work for a publisher and mainly did the history books. She still does the same sort of job, working from home with her computer. I love reading stories but history is stories that really happened and I like that better. So I read the stories and think what it must have been like to have lived then. At school they don't just want you to know what happened and when, they prefer you to think about why people might have done what they did: I like doing that.'

Lots of the others, especially the boys, called us swots because we enjoyed school work and did quite well in tests. Some of them pretended they were so clever that they knew all they needed to know and could concentrate on showing off to their mates. Poppy wasn't like that and I always tried to get a seat next to her on the bus but one day she wasn't at the bus stop.

She might have been ill but I thought it more likely that her Mum had gone to hospital to have the twins – they were due about now. When I got home I asked my Mum if she knew what had happened.

'Oh darling, it's terrible news. Poppy's Mum started bleeding and it didn't stop. Her Dad called an ambulance and the hospital did an operation straight away but they couldn't stop the bleeding and Poppy's Mum died. So did her baby boys.'

Mum was crying and I tried not to do the same and nearly succeeded but I didn't know what to say or what to do.

'Shall I go and see Poppy and tell her how sorry I am?'

Mum replied 'I'm not sure that's a good idea. She'll be ever so unhappy, probably feeling ill and won't really want to be polite to friends saying how sorry they are. It'll be bad for her Dad too, he won't be able to go to work but will have lots of arrangements to make and will be worrying about who can look after Poppy when he does go back to work.'

Mum's advice was 'I think the best thing is to wait a few days, we'll go to the funeral and that will give you a chance to see Poppy and be nice to her.'

*

The funeral was in a wood the other side of Cambridge and was so different from how my Grandad's funeral had been in a church. Some of the people who had known Poppy's Mum read poems or told stories about what they had done together. There wasn't a vicar to say she had been called home to live with God. The grave was already dug, the coffin put in and the soil pushed back, then Poppy and her Dad planted a tree on top of the grave while everyone walked round talking to each other about how they had known Poppy's Mum and what they might be able to do to help.

Eventually I got my turn to talk to Poppy:

'I think the tree is lovely. Will it have your Mum's name on it like a gravestone in a Church?'

'No, it's just for Daddy and me and we don't need a sign to remember her. We don't really need a tree either but we both think it will be nice, sometimes, to come back here and see how the tree is growing and sit under it and remember Mummy.'

She'd never called her "Mummy" when her Mum had been alive but that didn't seem the right thing to say.

Instead I tried 'I know another grave with trees, it's in the little wood where we had our sleep-out. It's got the ashes of the three brothers who used to own the farm, they are buried under a little cross with trees all round it. Would you like to come and see it?'

'I think I would, I haven't been out or talked to you since this happened. Can we go tomorrow?'

*

'Are you going out with Poppy?'

'Yes Mum, she said she wanted to.'

'Well take some food with you and have a snack if you get the chance, she might not be getting enough to eat with her Dad being so sad. Where are you going?' 'We might go along the Roman road again but it's Poppy's choice.' I didn't say anything about the grave in the nature reserve wood, in case Mum said it was a bad idea. I was pretty sure Poppy had said it was good idea. I got some biscuits and took some money too.

*

'Look, there it is Poppy, it's a bit like a grave in a churchyard. There's a wooden cross with a brass plate and their names on it. In the spring there's wild flowers all round and an old lady who was friends with them makes them a Christmas wreath.'

'Why are all three brothers in the same grave? Did they all die together in a car accident or something?'

'No, they died at different times, the dates are on the cross. They were cremated, not buried, and the last brother kept the ashes of the first two until he died himself. They didn't have wives or children so their friends in the village put the ashes of all three here, in a corner of the farm they had worked all their lives.'

'I think that's a lovely story and a very nice thing for the villagers to have done. I just want to read their grave post and think for a little while, then can we go for a walk?'

She did her thinking for quite a long time, so I nipped out to see if the sheep were OK in the field beside the wood. They were.

'Why don't we go down the Roman road again? It's not far from here and we can get to where we saw the fox.'

'And smelled the fox poo' she interrupted.

'Yes, it's not far to there, then there's a long bit of road we haven't explored yet.'

We soon got to where the fox had been but he wasn't there now, not even a whiff of his scent. I wondered if Poppy would start talking about the ancient Romans who had made this road but she wanted to talk about how we remembered people.

'I'm sorry for those brothers, they didn't have anyone to remember them – no children, no wives. When you die I think you sort-of stay alive while people remember you. That's what's important about Mummy's tree for me and Daddy.'

I replied 'They had lots of friends to remember them, that's wha made the grave and some still visit it and put flowers there. And the vicar was at the ceremony, I don't think they went to church much but maybe they got to heaven anyway.'

'I don't think anyone really believes in heaven any more. People go to church because they want to meet their friends or sing nice hymns. But when a young man is killed in a car crash do the people at the church say "Yippee, God's taken him to heaven early without him having to get old and lonely and dotty."? No, they're just like me, sad because they'll never see the person they loved again (because they don't really think there's a heaven for themselves either) and sad for the other people who have lost a friend or a husband. So all that really matters is memories to keep the person alive.'

'I think there's other ways of keeping memories alive. Children have got a bit of their parents in them and so have the grandchildren and great grandchildren. Before he died, my Grandad spent ages tracing his family tree, he found out a lot about the people who were part of our family hundreds of years ago: their names, what they did, where they lived and why one of them got hanged. He never knew those people but he could tell their stories and that made them live a bit too perhaps.'

'Yes, you're right. and I've just thought of another way you can live for ages after your dead – if people can read a book you wrote, or listen to music you composed or look at a picture you painted. The people who made this road knew that, one of Mummy's books about ancient Roman poetry has got this bit in it: the poet says something like "don't be sad when I'm dead and gone because I'll fly alive upon the lips of men". The only trouble is I can't remember who he was! I'll look him up when I get home.'

After a bit she changed the subject 'Oh, and why did your umpteen great grandad get hanged?'

'They said he was a highwayman. They were going to hang his girlfriend too but she was going to have a baby so they let her out of prison eventually. She had a son whose still got descendants now, I'm one of them.'

By now it was close to lunch time and we were a long way from home.

'Let's get some lunch in this pub.'

'Can children go in a pub and buy stuff?'

I think so, as long as they don't try and buy beer.' We each had a burger and a Coca-Cola.

As we ate Poppy thanked me 'Not just for the burger but for helping me think properly about Mummy and how to remember her. I know people get over being sad when someone dies but I'm afraid it will take ages. It's selfish but I'm sad about me too. Mum was my only real relation, she wasn't married when I was born, I never knew who my Dad was, my Dad now is my step-father. I wanted to be part of a bigger family when my baby brothers were born. Now it's just me and a Dad who is not my real Dad.'

I didn't know how to respond to Poppy's grief but eventually decided to say 'I'm an only child too. Mum and Dad wanted more kids but never had any. I'm lucky, I've got two parents but you are welcome to share them sometimes.'

'Can I have you as a brother?'

'Most of the boys with sisters say they are annoying. I'd rather have you has a friend. I hope you're that already.'

'Of course I am.'

She kissed me and said 'Sisters don't do that do they? And, again, thank you for the meal. I didn't know pubs did burgers and Coke, it's as good as McDonald's!'

'This is much more sophisticated.'

'Get you.'

'I shall be even more sophisticated and take you home in a hired carriage.' 'What do you mean?' 'There's a bus every two hours from here to our village and the next one comes in about ten minutes. There isn't a bus stop, you just wave at the bus and it stops.'

We were the only two on the bus and got home in a few minutes but it saved a long walk back along the Roman road. I think Poppy seemed a bit happier, maybe talking about being remembered had helped. And would she be more part of our family? She ran indoors to see how her Dad was doing and I went home to be asked by Mum what we had done. I told her some of it, mainly about the pub lunch and the bus ride home.

26

Chapter 3 – Finding Estonia

Everything began to settle down again. Poppy's Dad went back to work and she to school. There was the problem that her Dad had to leave for work at seven-thirty and didn't get home until six, so Mum and Dad asked her to come to us when her Dad left in the morning and then come home from school with me and stay until her Dad got back. I thought this was a great idea because it meant we could do our homework together, early, then I could settle down with my PlayStation or the television for the rest of the evening, after she'd gone home.

This went on for weeks and everyone at school stopped joking about "my girlfriend" and treated her as if she were my sister. I suppose I started to think that too but I wasn't sure I wanted to. I'd never had a sister but judging from the other boys they weren't a good idea. They were either older than you and bossed you about or younger than you and a nuisance when you wanted to play with your friends. Their only real advantage is you could see them in the bath and find-out what girls look like. Poppy was a real friend, the same age as me, unlike most real sisters, and she was someone I enjoyed talking with about interesting ideas. That didn't sound like a sister. What about the bath though?

By now it was the beginning of July. Soon we would be off for the long holiday in our cottage in France that we went to every year. What would happen to Poppy? Her Dad would be at work and she would be on her own in the house all day.

I asked Mum and Dad whether she could come with us.

'That's a lovely idea Moth but it depends on what her Dad thinks as well as what she wants.'

'Can I ask her and you ask him?' 'Alright, but be sure to tell her what it's like there. She might not like it.'

That evening, when we got back from school, I left Poppy doing her homework and went upstairs.

'Come up Poppy I want to show you something on the computer.'

'Got a new game?'

'No, look at this.'

I'd got Google Earth going before I'd called her. I'd found the image of our village and moved it to where I'd first met Poppy.

'Do you know where that is?'

'I don't think so.'

'I'll make the scale smaller, then you will.'

'Oh yes, that's our village and the nature reserve where the sheep live.'

'That's right, if I make the picture bigger again you can just about see the sheep.'

'Amazing, so you can.'

'Now I want to show you where I'm going on holiday.'

I typed the name of the village and the French post-code into Google. The photo zoomed out so you could see most of England and France, then homed-in on our bit of France, near the Pyrénées. It got bigger and bigger until you could see the individual houses in our hamlet and all the hay meadows and forest in the valley.

'We're there.'

'Which is your house, Moth?'

'This one. See all those meadows? That's where our neighbour keeps his cows and cuts his hay. He's only got about eight cows and milks them all by hand. He uses the milk to make really lovely cheese. There's all sorts of places to explore: old paths through the forest, little streams and the old mines. And French kids to play with. Would you like to come?'

'You bet I would but I'm worried about Daddy though, he still seems sad and he's been to the doctor to see if some pills will help. They haven't.'

'My Mum and Dad said they'd talk to your Dad, if you said you would like to spend the holiday with us. I hope he says "yes" and that you can come.'

Mum told me what Poppy's Dad had said. He thought it was a really good idea for her to go with us because it might help her get over everything and she deserved a good time. Also it would help him because he had been so worried about how he could look after Poppy and go to work at the same time. He'd already given us some money to pay for Poppy's food and things, so she's coming. 'Brilliant' was all I could think of to say.

There was a bit of a panic when her Dad couldn't find Poppy's passport and European health card and thought they might be lost or out of date. He found them in the end and they were all OK. Two days to go before we go.

*

The first bit of the journey is fun, we always get the ferry at Newhaven because it's quite cheap and takes you to Dieppe, which is closer to our cottage than Calais is. Dad likes to avoid the French motorways when he can, because you have to pay for them, but he usually uses them for part of the journey. That meant I could show Poppy how you get a ticket from the machine when you join the motorway and then you put the ticket in another machine when you leave and it tells you how much to pay. French drivers can do that through their car window but an English car has the driver on the wrong side, so we helped by getting the tickets and paying the tolls with Dad's bank card. You don't need to know his PIN number.

The journey goes on and on. It takes about twelve hours to get from Dieppe to our place, with Mum and Dad sharing the driving. Dad knew we'd get bored and had invented a game for us. He'd printed off some Internet pages that had pictures of all the different Euro coins from all the countries that use them, not just the Euros but the two Euro coins right down to the one centimes. You can use coins from any of the Euro countries in France. Dad gave us a bag of small change and challenged us to find coins from as many countries as we could. The game lasted a long time because every time we stopped for petrol or a snack Dad paid with €50 notes and got lots more coins in the change.

We soon had a big pile of coins from France and quite big ones from Spain, Germany and Italy. I was quite pleased when I found one from Portugal, then Poppy got an Irish one: they are really rare. 'Sensible country, Ireland, I wish we used the Euro' said Dad.

Poppy was looking through all the countries that used Euros.

'I want to find one from Estonia – I'm not even sure where it is.'

'It's right up north near Finland' said Dad, still being a teacher even on holiday.

I said 'I don't suppose many people live in Estonia and hardly any will come right down here to spend their Euros. I bet we don't find one.'

Poppy wasn't convinced 'The Euros can come on their own, they don't need an Estonian to bring them. I bet lots of Estonians go to Germany and spend Euros. Then a German might visit here and spend an Estonian Euro.'

It sounded perfectly logical but we never did find an Estonian Euro.

Poppy was becoming an historian again.

'Do you think Roman coins moved round Europe when it was the Roman Empire? Perhaps that coin they found where your sheep live was made in Rome. At least in those days England used the same coins as everyone else.'

'I don't think the Romans gave us much choice about that, no silly politicians refusing to join the Eurozone' said Dad.

At last we were nearly there and turned off the little road by the river in the bottom of our valley to go up the winding track that eventually led to our house. It was already getting quite dark and suddenly two deer ran across in front of us. Poppy asked me what sort they were.

'Roe deer, they are the commonest here. We've mostly got Fallow and Muntjac at home but Roe are rare where we live.'

We were there, Mum unlocked the door and we started carrying stuff in.

'We need to get you two into bed, it's ever so late.'

We always left some beds ready made-up with clean duvet covers and sheets, so it would be easy when we came next time.

'OK you two, you can share the blue room with the bunk beds. Just get in your pyjamas and go to sleep. We'll show you everything tomorrow.'

It wasn't quite that quick: we had to choose who had the top bunk (Poppy) and I had to show her where the loo and the bathroom were. She took her pyjamas into the bathroom and came back ready for bed, so I did the same.

I didn't get to sleep straight away, the only time I'd slept with Poppy we'd been next to each other in our straw hut, kissing and talking about willies.

Now she was a metre above me and hadn't even kissed me good night.

We woke up early. Poppy wanted to see where we were and I wanted to show her. There's something nice about showing people a place you know about and love. You have to think how to describe everything and so you remember when you first knew the places. We hadn't just discovered everywhere, we'd given them names when there didn't seem to be any French names that the people round here used.

'Let's go to the shower-bath, it's just along the road.'

'I've just had a shower.'

'It's not a real shower, that's just what we call it.'

At the first sharp bend on the road out of the village was the little waterfall where the water is spread out by all the plants growing in the moisture and the water runs down the leaves and sprinkles in a shower. Just next to the waterfall is a spring and the water is collected into a little tank made of stones cemented together. There's a tap and you can use it to get a drink. The water's lovely, much nicer than the plastic-bottled stuff they sell in supermarkets.

'Can we go back and get a bottle for the water?'

'We can do that for lunch-time and pick some of that cress there on the wet rocks, it makes lovely soup. I want to show you the iron tadpoles.'

I'd expected some joke about iron tadpoles but she pretended she knew what I meant and just walked with me along to the next bend in the road where there was another little waterfall, much smaller than the shower-bath.

'Look, you see where the water is running over the rock? It's all red and rusty. The rock is full of iron, there used to be an iron mine down in the valley. The rusty water runs into a big puddle at the edge of the road and that's where the iron tadpoles live. Look, there they are. They don't seem to mind the iron but they don't turn into frogs as quickly as the ones in clean water.'

We went back and got two bottles for water and a bag for some cress. Cold from the fridge, Mum and Dad said the water was even better than the wine they usually had with lunch.

'Where can we go next?'

'Well, there's the salamander stream where you can find salamander tadpoles sometimes or we could go and find all the farm animals.'

'Let's do that.'

Finding the cows was easy, you could see them in the field below the village but it was best to go down a little track beside the fields to get to the place where a gate let you through the electric fence without getting a shock. They were light brown cows, six of them. Étienne herded them up the track every evening to milk them. He and Christianne milked them by hand and then made the milk into really good, soft, smelly cheese. The cows spent the night in a field near the village and then went down to their daytime pasture after the morning milking.

'Are there any more cows, six doesn't seem many?'

'There are some somewhere, these are the only ones giving milk at the moment I think.'

We climbed back to the village and down the road until it turned into a tractor track below the village.

'There's usually some animals in the fields down here.'

There were: the other cows, two full-sized and two young ones.

'They're heifers – young cows that haven't had their first calf yet.'

'Where's the bull? Is he dangerous?'

'No he's not here, I think it's the vet that keeps all the bulls round here. When it's the right time for the cows to get pregnant he brings the bull's stuff and puts it inside the cow and the calf starts growing.'

'If I were a cow I'd rather meet the bull I think. I'd like to know the father of my child.'

I was about to say that I'd think the same way, if I were a bull, but decided not to.

In the next field, right over the far side almost hidden in the shade of the bushes, were the donkeys. Three of them, a young one, a mother and her really young baby. Poppy wanted it as a pet.

'Does Étienne milk his donkeys?'

'No, I think they're mainly pets though they do some work pulling carts sometimes but some people round here milk donkeys. In the market on Saturdays you can buy soap made from donkey milk.'

'Can we go and buy some? It would be like being Cleopatra, having a bath of asses milk. We'd only have soap though – how much is a bath full of asses milk?'

'I've no idea but we'll go to the market and you can ask.'

Last of all we found the goats, they were new to me too, Étienne had started making goat cheese as well as the cow cheese. There was a proper family of goats: three nannies, two kids and a big handsome billy. I really liked the look of him. At least the nanny goats don't have to wait for the vet.

It was Thursday.

'It's two days before the market, so tomorrow I'll ask Mum and Dad if I can drive you to the Top of the World.'

'But you can't drive. Where's the Top of the World?'

'Wait and see.'

Dad had let me drive the car on the little forest tracks since I was really small. I'd sit on his lap and do the steering wheel, while he did everything else. Now I was big enough to change gear and brake properly and it was really fun. Dad sat beside me, in case I did anything silly but I didn't.

When we'd turned on to the forest track Dad stopped, to let me take the driver's seat.

Poppy asked 'Wasn't that a no entry sign we just passed?'

'Yes but it said "sauf ayant droit" which means you can use the track if you've got the right to and everyone who lives in the valley has.'

So I started slowly up the track and struggled a bit to turn the steering wheel fast enough to get round all the really sharp bends. "Hairpin-circle-bends" I used to call them when I was a little kid.

'My ears have gone pop' said Poppy from the back of the car.

'So have mine, they always do when you climb up high.'

We got to the top where there was a place for the big lorries to park when they were cutting down the trees, but no one was there today. The Top of the World is higher than the other side of our valley, so we could see right across and over the hills to the flat farmland beyond.

'Look Poppy, you can just see the edge of the town where they have the market.'

While we were trying to count all the hamlets scattered up the sides of our valley, and see which of them had people living in them, Mum had got the picnic out.

Dad said he wanted to get home to try and mend the washing machine which had started to leak. Did we want to come or walk home?

I said 'Let's walk' and Poppy said 'It's miles along that road but at least it'll be downhill.'

So Mum and Dad went home, making sure we had our phones with us and saying not to go in any of the old mines.

'We don't have to walk along the road, Poppy. There's a nearly secret path the hunters use in autumn. It goes straight down the ridge near the old mines that we mustn't go in.'

'OK let's be hunters, not miners. What shall we hunt?'

'Wild Boar of course, like Asterix.'

'Do you ever see them?'

'Yes, sometimes. They're supposed to be really fierce but they always run away as fast as they can. I think they're fierce when the hunters' dogs catch them though.'

'I don't want to be a hunter now, let's be David Attenborough and film them. Will they let you tickle their backs like you can farm pigs?'

'I've never got close enough to try.'

The hunters' path started at the second corner on the road and went up a bit until it got to what was almost a cliff, looking down into a valley that was completely wooded. No fields nor houses anywhere.

'That's the Secret Valley, Poppy. You can get into it from down near our house but not from up here.'

Now the path turned down hill and ran right beside the cliff above the Secret Valley. After a bit we came to a tree house, I'd seen it before and knew what it was.

'The hunter's made that. Let's climb up and you can see the cage where they keep their tame pigeons that attract the wild ones to be shot.'

'How horrid, don't the shot pigeons just fall over the edge into the Secret Valley?'

'I suppose the hunting dogs go and get them if they do.'

I really wanted to show Poppy some boar and at last I thought we might be lucky.

'Listen. There's something rustling over there under those bushes.'

It was a boar, a mother with three stripey babies but they all disappeared, squeaking and grunting, as soon as they saw us.

'That was lovely, I don't think David Attenborough got much film though, I tried to get my phone out but they were gone as soon as we saw them.'

We went on down and came to a junction where a path ran left, away from the cliff-edge path.

'That's the path that will get us home, come on.'

'Who made all these paths, they must have been proper roads almost, once upon a time.'

'They were, I think, there were lots of people who worked in the mines a hundred years ago. We think our house was used by a mining family. They probably did farming in the summer and mining in the winter.'

I added 'Those mines are ever so old. In the local museum, there's bits of a big Roman wine jar. It was found in the mine near our house.'

'So this is a Roman road like ours in England. It's not very straight though' said Poppy.

'It must be impossible to make straight roads across river valleys like this. I wonder if Romans could walk all the way to Estonia from here.'

'I'm sure they never got near there, I don't think their empire went further than the edge of Germany.'

'Perhaps we'll get to visit Estonia one day.'

'Not for ages I hope, I want to find out all about here first.'

Chapter 4 – Our Grandads Lived Here

That evening, when Dad was feeling pleased because he had mended the washing machine, I asked him if we could take Poppy to Niaux. We'd been there several times and loved it, I was sure she would too.

'That's a great idea, Moth. I'll go online and make a booking for tomorrow afternoon if I can.' And he could. 'Don't tell Poppy yet, it's a surprise.'

*

Today was Saturday so we started really early and got to the market while there were still some places to park and things to buy. It's one of my favourite places because it's so different from England and I can feel a bit French and chat to the stall holders. Poppy wanted a bath full of asses milk and found the stall where she bought two bars of asses soap (the donkey-milkers speak English so she didn't need my help).

There were lots of stalls selling things that weren't food: old clothes, old books, new mattresses, plus stalls with foreign carvings and jewellery, being sold by people from far-off countries. But what I liked best were the food stalls, mostly being run by the people who grew the things themselves: lots of vegetables, skinned rabbits, dried sausages, wild yellow toadstools called girolles and lots of different cheeses.

'Why isn't it like this at home?' asked Poppy. 'I suppose it's because everyone goes to Tesco or Aldi' she continued.

I replied 'I don't think so, this town's got three big supermarkets like Tesco, two cheap ones like Aldi and several small local ones too. There are still little shops selling really good food at higher prices. It's just because people like the market and take the time to shop here, meet their friends and have lunch with them. It's a whole way of life.'

'And also the farming's all different' I went on. 'At home almost all the farms grow fields of rape or wheat – who wants to eat that? You hardly ever find a cow or an orchard or vegetables you could sell in the market. The farmers are ever so rich and want to keep you off their land and out of their pheasant woods. Here there are lots of farmers with small farms and old cars and long hair. They don't mind if you go on their land and they sell most of what they grow at the market. I remember once, trying to read the lonely hearts column in the local paper, there was an advert that said "farmer 30 with 20 hectares would like to meet young lady with tractor". I don't think you'd see that in England and I'm almost sure it wasn't a joke.'

We didn't get our lunch at the market, it was too early, so we set off for the drive towards Poppy's surprise. The road had been going up for some time but at last it started going down again and we could see the first big town we'd come to since leaving the market.

Suddenly Poppy cried 'Look at that castle, it's like a fairy tale one.'

The castle has three towers, one round and two square. It's got a museum inside but it was closed for renovations and anyway we wouldn't have time to see it today.

I told Poppy 'The most famous man who lived there was Gaston Phoebus, Count of Foix. He was really keen on hunting but spent most of his time fighting. Foix was a little country all on its own and it was the time when our Black Prince was fighting the French nearby. Phoebus was cunning, sometimes on one side sometimes the other.'

Poppy knew when the Black Prince had lived, which is more than I did. 'That must have about six hundred and fifty years ago.'

We stopped in Foix to have some lunch. We always went to the same cheap restaurant below the castle. It's in an old building where you can see all the timbers on the outside, like lots of the old houses where we lived in England. The restaurant man greeted Mum and Dad like old friends and sat us down at a table outside the restaurant in the shade. No cars were allowed along the road, so it was the nicest place to be.

'What can we have to eat?' asked Poppy.

'You don't really get much choice at lunchtimes, he makes lots of the same thing and does it really well. So you either eat it or not. You'll like it, whatever it is.'

There was a starter with lots of salad, slices of boiled egg and dry sausage, then a couscous with bits of chicken and an ice-cream for pudding.

The one thing you could choose was what colour wine you wanted but children didn't have to have wine. When he'd found out that Dad wanted red wine and Mum white, he turned to me and said:

'Et pour toi et ta soeur, mon vieux?' and I said 'S'il vous plait, du coca dans une verre sucré pour moi et mon amie: elle n'est pas ma soeur.'

It was a good chance to show off my French.

'What did you order?' asked Poppy.

'Something I've always had here since I was about six. He thought you were my sister and I told him you weren't.'

The "somethings" soon arrived: just Coca-Cola in tall glasses which had had their lips dipped in wet sugar and left so the sugar dried on. Lovely. But maybe I'm getting too old for drinks like that, they are not very sophisticated.

After lunch there was still a little while before we had to be at Niaux for our visit, so Mum and Dad took us to the bookshop where we could look at some books with pictures of Gaston Phoebus. Poppy fell in love with a book full of coloured pictures of hunting scenes. The text described how to hunt each kind of animal and had been written by Gaston Phoebus himself. It had been translated into modern French but the coloured pictures were exact copies of the original book. Poppy counted her holiday money and decided to buy it and when I read it next day I was very pleased she had.

We travelled on down the main road towards Andorra.

'Isn't that still a little country that's all on its own, like Foix used to be?' asked Poppy and Dad said 'Yes.'

We soon turned off the main road and followed the signs to Niaux, the car park is inside the entrance to a cave. While Dad went to buy our tickets and find out which group we were going with, I explained to Poppy 'We're going in a cave where cavemen lived and painted the animals they hunted.'

There were two other English families and one lot of Germans who spoke good English to us. When the guide came he gave us each a big torch and explained we were going to walk through a long tunnel until we got to the "Salon Noir" where the paintings were. As we walked he was explaining lots of things in French and I tried to show off by translating some of it to Poppy. I should have left it to Dad because I got some things wrong and the guide stopped and corrected me in perfectly good English. Then he went back to French even though the whole group spoke English and only a few of us understood French.

We were told to turn off our torches when we got to the Salon Noir, so it was completely dark until the guide turned on his torch and started to show us the paintings: beautiful pictures of bison, wild horses, deer and bouquetin (I think they are called ibex in English). He told us it was still the Ice Age but starting to warm up a bit when the paintings were made: it would have been like living in the north of Norway today. About 12,000 years ago the people who made the paintings were just like us, not like cartoon cavemen. If you could magic one of their babies to grow up in a French family today he would go to school and use a mobile phone and no one would know he was a caveman who would never even have used an iron pot if he'd stayed at home in his cave.

On the way home Poppy was full of questions most of which we couldn't answer. 'Why did they go right down there in the dark to do the paintings?' Eventually she homed in on they idea that the cavemen were just like us.

'If it was cold then, in southern France, it must have been impossible to live in England. I expect the cavemen moved north when it got warmer and some of them might be my grandparents a few greats back.'

I asked how many "Greats" and, being Poppy, she said 'Let's work it out. How much older is your Dad than you?'

'Twenty-five years, but what's that got to do with it? He's not a caveman.'

I could hear Mum trying not to laugh in the front seat.

'It means a generation is about twenty-five years, go back fifty years and you meet Grandad when he was your age and a hundred years to meet Great, Great Grandad when he was that age. The cave painters lived 12,000 years ago so that's 480 generations, 480 Greats Grandad.'

Mum wasn't laughing now, she was interested and obviously quite impressed. So was I.

'Do you think one of the cave painters in Niaux was one of my 480 Great Grandads? It doesn't seem very likely, there were probably only a few people who lived in that cave.'

Poppy knew I was wrong. 'I bet they were nearly all your grandparents and mine too, at least those who didn't die before they'd had any children. How many grandparents did you have?' 'Four, before one grandad died.'

'How many great grandparents?' 'I don't know, I never met them.'

Dad chipped in and said I'd had eight.

'That's how it works' said Poppy 'one of you, two parents, four grandparents, eight great-grand parents: it doubles every generation. Try doubling one for 480 times and you get a huge number, billions of billions. So anyone who was alive then was probably a grandparent for both of us and everyone else in Europe.'

That seemed a very big idea and I needed to think about it and was quiet for the rest of the way home, while Poppy got out her new book and looked at the paintings of the hunted animals. Those hunts happened only about 650 years ago. Twenty-six generations. How many grandads did I have then? Was I the 26th great grandson of Gaston Phoebus? Poppy would soon want me to translate the instructions on how to catch bears – I'd better start thinking in French again and leave the maths to Poppy.

Chapter 5 – Visiting Narnia

Philippe and Emilie had been here for some time and we spent most days playing with them. It was hot and they had a swimming pool. One day we walked down the path which had, in the days when the miners lived here, been the only road to our hamlet. Under the dark trees it was a muddy path but when it was out in the sun, going through bracken patches that had once been farm fields, it became a rather prickly one. At the bottom we got to the motor road and the river.

'Let's go looking for gold' suggested Philippe.

All the rivers round here have gold in them but not very much, there seems to have been lots in Roman times but they probably stole most of it. Anyway, it was a great excuse to get in the river. None of us had brought any swimming stuff but no one seemed to mind, not even the people in cars who waved as they went by.

We found some little specks of gold but Emilie said it wasn't, it was bits of copper or fool's gold or something. So we lay down in the sun, got dry and dressed then started down the valley to go home a different way.

'Look at that house, it's not very pretty is it? We used to call it the horrible house. It was one of three schools in the valley – they're all closed now but children from our hamlet used to walk all the way down the hill every morning and back up the hill in the evening.'

We'd been talking in French all day and it was only a few times that Poppy had asked me what someone had said. She didn't say much herself but was starting to understand quite a lot.

When we'd got back up the hill that was the shortest and steepest way to our village from the river, the way the children would once have come home from school, we needed a Coca-Cola each and Philippe and Emilie's Mum gave us some.

'We're going away for about a week to see my sister, come and have a meal with us when we get back.'

So we were on our own, apart from Étienne and Christianne but they were both busy making hay and milking cows. Dad said 'Would you like to walk to Spain?'

'Isn't it miles and miles and you have to climb mountains?'

'It's not that bad, you can get quite close to the border in a car, then you climb a bit of a mountain track to the border and after that it's down hill all the way to Spain. It's one of the ways people used to escape from the Germans during the war. When you get to the first Spanish village you can wait until either Mum or I have driven the car round to get you back home.'

It sounded a really great explore and we both said 'yes please' straight away.

We got ready in the evening so we could start early next day. We each had a haversack with some picnic things. Dad said 'You don't really need water, it's jolly heavy and there are plenty of little springs.' So we just packed a light plastic waterproof and a few spare clothes, in case we got wet anyway. Of course Mum checked we all had our phones fully charged in case anyone got lost.

The track up to the border was really rutted and our car only just made-it up to the little car-park, which was as far as ordinary people were allowed to go. There was a locked gate across the track and Dad said only the farmers who had their sheep up there, or the scientists who studied the wild animals in the nature reserve, were allowed to drive up. 'I bet they've got Land Rovers, not a car like ours.'

We went through the little gap beside the locked gate and started our climb. Soon we came to a whole field full of sheep-folds. 'That's where they round up the sheep in autumn before the lorries come to take them all down to their winter quarters' explained Dad.

We soon got to the first of several blue lakes beside the road. It was hot and the water must be lovely and cool.

'Mum, can we...'

'No, we need to get on if we are going to get to Spain today.'

It was picnic time when we got to the border.

'Look over there' said Dad 'all those holes are made by marmots. If you are quiet and still while you eat your lunch you'll probably see some. I want you to stay here on your own for a while. Mum and I want to try and find somewhere we had a picnic once, up here on our first holiday together, in the Spring before we were married. Is that OK?'

Of course it was and I wondered if Poppy and I would want to come back here in years to come.

When they'd gone, I told Poppy 'I think Dad had a bottle of wine in his haversack.'

'I suppose you can't rely on finding wine springs up here' she replied.

The marmots did come out and Poppy thought they were sweet: 'Like big friendly guinea-pigs. They keep taking grass into their burrows and whistle at each other.'

Suddenly they all whistled at the same time and shot back down their holes. A huge bird circled overhead trying to see if any marmots were still above ground. They were all safe and the bird, I think it was a golden eagle, glided away without flapping its wings at all.

We didn't think the marmots would come out again for ages, so we finished our picnic and went to the edge of the steep slope that led down into Spain. We were both fascinated by what we could see, we were so high-up and looking down on a whole little country that didn't know we were up here watching. Two men and a dog were moving some sheep from one field to another. In another field a whole family was cutting hay.

'Look, Moth, they're using scythes not tractors, I thought it was a hundred years ago people did that.'

We watched. It wasn't like we were part of what we saw. It was a different world and a different time and we might have been watching them on Google Earth for all they knew.

Suddenly I knew what it was really like 'Poppy, did you ever read the Silver Chair – it's one of the Narnia books?'

'Yes, I loved those books. They're fairy stories of course. I know some of the stories were nicked from the Bible but you don't have to believe the Bible or a fairy tale to enjoy it and know it's a good story.'

'Well, remember the start of the story: Jill and Eustace had escaped from their horrible school by magic and were sitting at the top of a high cliff in Aslan's country, looking down on Narnia miles away below them. Aslan's country wasn't part of Narnia, it was outside and they weren't part of it till Aslan came and floated them down by magic. I think this is Aslan's country and down there, where we're going, is Narnia.'

'I hope we meet the Marsh Wiggle' she said.

It wasn't Aslan that came to lead us into Narnia, it was Mum and Dad. They must have been glad to see us and they looked very pleased with themselves.

They had decided it would be Dad who went back and drove the car to Spain while Mum led us to Spain the quicker, on-foot, way. Sometimes the mountainside was so steep you had to zig-zag to get down. There were paths that looked like they went somewhere but kept turning out to be sheep tracks that just went nowhere useful at all.

Eventually the land got flatter and we were in hot fields instead of being on the side of a mountain. There were butterflies, lots and lots of them, including Marbled Whites that must have been Spanish Marbled Whites – much less black on them than the sort that live in France and England.

I was creeping up on Marbled Whites, trying to get a good bit of film on my phone, when the thunder started. It was really sudden, a flash of lightning then a clap of thunder almost straight way.

'That means it's really close.' I told Poppy.

'You don't need to explain that – and look at all that rain coming.'

The rain just hit us and the drops were so big and so fast falling that they almost hurt. It was too late to get waterproofs out of our haversacks.

Mum spotted a stone barn and it was empty:

'Quick, in here.' We stood there dripping. 'It's no good, we shan't get dry like this. We'll have to take off all these wet things, use them like damp towels, to get as dry as we can, then put on our dry stuff.'

We were standing there, trying to get drier, when Poppy asked 'Why doesn't this ever happen in books? Jill and Eustace never stripped off, they never even went for a wee. I don't think the Marsh Wiggle would have approved – well he didn't approve of anything really.'

Mum was in the corner of the barn and trying to be more like a Marsh Wiggle than a Mother.

We were all dry and properly dressed when Dad phoned to check where we were and take us to get a good meal in a nice dry Spanish restaurant.

Chapter 6 – The Télécabine and what it led to

It was going to be Poppy's birthday at the end of next week; she would be twelve, one of the youngest in our class. I'd been twelve since February. Dad asked her what she would like as a birthday treat. She thought for a bit and said 'Is there anywhere we could get really good views of the stars? Maybe somewhere with a telescope to see them really well?' Dad said he thought there was but that it would be really difficult to get a ticket because people booked up long in advance. He would make some enquiries.

That evening I asked Poppy if she would like to walk along the road, past the iron tadpoles, before we went to bed. You could get good views of the stars and it would be something to do until Dad had got some tickets for a real observatory. We've got a sort of star-chart that you turn to today's date and time and it shows you a picture of what stars you should be able to see. It was a nice clear night and dark enough to see the stars really well.

I told Poppy:'It's much better than England but there's still too many street lights about. Look at that little hamlet across the valley, I went there once. It's got three street lights and three houses and no one lives in any of them.'

Poppy got out the star-chart disk and set the time.

'Look over there, that's the Great Bear that we saw in England.'

'What's that W-shaped group up there?' 'It must be Cassiopeia, I've never seen it so well when I was in England.'

Then she wanted to find as many of the birthday star signs as she could: Aries, Taurus, Virgo and that lot. They are really hard to sort out and I can't imagine how the ancients saw any pictures of things in those groups of stars.

Suddenly there was a shooting star burning so briefly as it shot across the sky. We both saw it but only just.

'A falling star' she said wistfully.

'Shall we go and find out where it came down?'

'Don't be silly, they are just little bits of space dust that burn up before they hit the ground.'

'I'll show you where it came down, come on.'

She came on but she seemed pretty certain I was playing a trick.

I took her back towards the iron tadpoles where there was a rock with some brambles growing over it.

'Look, there it is, your fallen star.'

There was a steady greenish glowing star under the bush and she was almost convinced I was telling the truth. She crouched down to look at it.

'You rotten pig, it's an insect!'

'It's a glow-worm, I think they're interesting and I can always find them here. They eat snails and the glowing ones can't fly. They're the females.'

'Like your March Moths, poor things. It's only the males get to fly and have fun.'

I ignored her and went on 'The males only have tiny little glows, they're fireflies and when one sees a female's bright light he comes down and they both have some fun. You don't often find them in England, I think it's because there's so many street lights that the males and females hardly ever meet.'

After her biology lesson, we both went home to bed. We were still in the blue room with the bunk beds. When we'd done our teeth and climbed into our bunks she got out a torch and turned it on.

'What are you doing?'

'Just glowing.'

*

Dad had been successful. Poppy's treat was to go to the observatory on the top of the Pic du Midi about seventy miles from us. You had to go up the mountain in télécabines and it was easy to get tickets to go up in the daytime. But if you were lucky enough to get a reservation you can stay overnight and see the big telescopes working and get good views of the stars yourself.

Dad said 'We were very lucky, I know someone who used to work there. He got us permission to use a couple of the old staff rooms. The proper tourist rooms are much more posh and expensive and they were all full anyway. Our two rooms were cheaper but they aren't very close together. It doesn't matter, when we've been up half the night watching stars, no one's going to worry about where they sleep.'

There weren't all that many people waiting to go up in the télécabine. Lots of daytime visitors were coming down after their visit was over, then we climbed in to go up. When it starts, the télécabine goes over one of the supports that hold up the cables and it jerks. It scared everyone the first time and they gasped or squeaked. Then we were hanging about a hundred metres up, over a gulley in the mountain, and looking down. Some people squeaked there too. When we landed at the top we found it wasn't the top, you had to get out and go in a second télécabine up to the real top.

When we had really landed and one of the staff showed us where our rooms were, Dad told us to come to the restaurant we'd seen, as soon as we'd dumped our stuff and had a wash if we wanted one.

'Look, it's got a double bed.'

'I don't mind if you don't. Will it be OK?'

'It's not much different from bunk beds is it?'

It was quite a posh restaurant and we had one of those long meals with lots of courses and time between the courses to chat, it was just the sort of meal the French are so good at. Afterwards they told us it was time to visit the planetarium. It was a bit of a disappointment really, a bit like a cinema inside a giant ball and the film showed the history of the observatory and pictures of the stars projected on the curved walls of the planetarium.

It was hot and the commentary went on and on and I couldn't follow it all. I looked at Poppy and she couldn't understand any of it. It wasn't long before she'd gone to sleep and I soon heard some adult snores from a few rows away. When I woke up it was over and time to go and see the real stars and telescopes.

'Is it in that tall metal tower over there?'

Dad explained 'No Poppy, that's a television tower, half the people in southern France watch programmes that are transmitted from here.'

The real telescope was in a sort of room a bit like the planetarium. They could open the roof so the telescope could look out and see the sky. I thought it would be a big version of one of those toy telescopes you open out and look through with one eye but it wasn't. There were wires all over the place and controls so the telescope could be made to twist round and look at just what you wanted. The picture was on a big screen, like a television, and they recorded the pictures so the scientists could study them later and see whether any of the stars wobbled or were going to blow up.

The best bit was when they pointed the telescope at the planets in our solar system: Jupiter with its red spot, Saturn with its rings and Mars. We didn't see Venus or the other planets The telescope made them look really big and you could see the details, whereas the stars were just different-sized points of light.

It was all over much to soon and we had to go to bed, it was well after midnight but I didn't think I'd sleep. I'd slept enough in the planetarium and so had Poppy.

'What did you like best Poppy?'

'Oh the planets, definitely.'

'Me too, but if you think about it, what we could see wasn't nearly as clear and detailed as the photos of the planets that were taken close-up by those American spaceships and sent back to Earth by radio.'

Poppy thought about this for a bit and said 'You're right of course but this was better because it was real, we were kind of part of it, because we were there and watching. Remember when we saw the fox on the Roman road? It was a long way off and we only saw it catch a vole. If we'd watched a film about foxes, we'd have seen it really close-up and seen her feed the vole to the cubs. We'd have seen more, but what we saw was better, we were there with the fox and we even smelt it.'

'I know just what you mean but I don't think I did before you explained about the fox.' We both thought a bit more.

'Time for bed, Poppy.'

She didn't feel like the day was over any more than I did.

'I want a shower. The shower is over there in the corner but there's no curtain, I shan't mind if you watch.'

'I want a shower too, you first.'

'Let's shower together, it'll be fun.'

It was, especially when I soaped her and smoothed the soap over her breasts. They weren't very big but lovely and soft and her nipples went quite hard. Then she soaped me and that was nice too.

We found some towels and dried each other, then lay on the bed looking at the ceiling. After a short while we each seemed to decide at the same moment to turn on our sides and look at each other.

'Do you remember the question I asked the night we first met?'

'Of course I do.'

'Well, I remember your answer. Now you've had a good look, do you want one?' 'Yours is very nice, but I've got my own, though it's not very big.'

'What do you mean, I can't see anything.'

'It's hidden inside the lips. It's easier to feel it than see it and it feels nice when I touch it. Give me your hand and I'll show you.'

It felt a bit damp and a bit hard but not much like a real willy.

'Do you wee through it?'

'No, it's not much use at all really, a bit like your nipples.'

'Do you call it a willy?'

'Mummy said that is what it is really. She told me all about things and how my body was going to change as I got older. Boys are really lucky because their bits have nice simple names and no one really minds if you say "cock" or "balls" in the playground. Girls' bits mostly have the sort of names a doctor would use or you can find in the diagrams in biology books. My willy is really called a clitoris but I wish it were called a willy. The only everyday name for a girl's bits is so horrid that it's almost as bad as saying "nigger" in the playground. Even then you don't know what bit someone's talking about, they are probably just being horridly rude to another boy.'

This was getting a bit embarrassing, girl's bits were interesting though. Very interesting.

'Did you mind, that first night, when I asked you about willies?'

'Of course not, I knew you would.' 'How did you know?'

'Well, you ran off with Jacob shouting about wild wees and peeing up a tree. I wanted to watch and heard everything you said. You were going to ask that question soon enough. I had my answer ready.'

Next morning, over breakfast in the restaurant, Mum and Dad asked whether we'd been able to sleep alright.

Poppy chipped in quickly 'It was so exciting last night, we talked for quite a long time before we went to sleep but it was all worth it, we've had a lovely time and I've had a super birthday present.'

They seemed very pleased with that little speech but I looked at Poppy and she smiled.

Chapter 7 – The Juniper Rock

The next day we started out for a walk to the iron tadpoles but we'd only got to the corner, where the village dustbins are, when I thought of something else.

'Come on Poppy, let's go up here, I've got something I want to show you.'

'I've already seen it' she said smiling.

'Only on Google' I replied.

You can't really see the path where it starts beside the dustbins but as soon as you've pushed through a bush you are on an old track that the miners used, on their way to the silver mine just above the village. After quite a long climb we got to an open rocky place with a big bush on it shaped like a Christmas tree.

'That's a juniper tree and we call this the Juniper Rock. Down there is the Salamander Stream and all the scree is where the miners dumped the rocks that weren't silver ore but look down there, you can see all the houses in the village, well their roofs anyway. That's what I meant by showing you something you'd only seen on Google.'

'It's not like being above Narnia on the edge of Spain is it? We're still low down and part of this place. Like you always will be I think, you're happy here. You know every corner, all the history, the names of the cows and can talk to everyone. It's not like England where no one is really part of the village. People go off to work in Cambridge or

London everyday and keep their doors locked and their children indoors. Here all the doors are open and you can just shout "Salut" and walk in. Even the people in the market know you. When did you last meet a friend on the checkout in Tesco?'

She seemed to be able to say how I felt better than I could myself.

'You're right, I'm part of this place and don't ever want to lose it. I'm not the sort of person who wants to keep running off to a different holiday place every year. Going to the same one is going home and this is a better home than where we live in England.'

I remembered something 'Once Dad was driving into a little village we hadn't been to before. There was a home-made sign panel beside the road and Dad laughed when he saw it.'

'What did it say?'

'Ralentir, nos enfants sont élevées en liberté.'

'Well I know "Ralentir" means slow down and there's something about children. What does "élevées en liberté" mean?'

'It's what they put on the side of a dead chicken in Intermarché. It means "free-range". That's what I've always felt like here.'

'Like a dead chicken?'

'No, free-range, left in safety to live my own life and explore things. Every childhood should be like that but too many kids in England don't even want it to be. Often their parents are worse.'

'Will you live here all the time when you're grown-up?'

'I'd like to but I'm not sure what I could do. I want to study moths but I think it would be difficult to get a university or something to pay me to do it here. I wondered whether I could live here and use the internet to teach French to Australian children in the Outback. I might just keep cows and make cheese, I think I would be happy doing that, I don't want to be rich. Perhaps I could write a book.'

'Do a book: I love books, let's start now, I'll help. I won't be much use if it's a book about moths though.'

'No, I think it will have to be a novel.'

'But then you need a really exciting story, can you invent one?'

'I don't think it has to be exciting, just interesting. You don't have to make it all up, you just take interesting things that have happened to you and your friends and string them together to make a story. You can change the people things happen to and make-up some bits. Oh, and you have to change the names of the people.'

'So is it about us?'

'I suppose it might be, will I be able to put in what happened on the Pic du Midi?'

'Only if you change my name.'

'I'll call you Poppy.'

'That's my middle name.'

'Well hardly anyone knows that.'

Next day we went to the Juniper Rock again. There was something I wanted to ask Poppy about and I thought it might be less difficult up there.

She'd been especially good at understanding things yesterday.

'Are we going to get your book started?'

'Not yet. Do you remember after we had that shower at the Pic du Midi?'

'Of course I do.'

'Well, I think we should talk about ourselves and each other. Living in the same house and sort of sharing a Mum and Dad, is like being a brother and sister. Most brothers and sisters I know kind of like each other but treat each other quite differently from their own friends. We're only twelve and most of my mates talk about having girlfriends but their important friends are still boys like them.'

She didn't say anything, so I went on 'It's weird for us, my Mum and Dad aren't yours even though we share a house and a bedroom. You haven't got a Mum any more and you have no idea who your Dad is. I think you love your step-Dad but he has to work and can't easily look after you as well, unless he finds someone else to marry pretty quick. Do you want a nice step-Dad and a new step-Mum? Or would you like to be part of my family? If you were would you be my sister? Or something better?'

Poppy thought a bit and replied 'I'd love being part of your family for ever but what we did at the Pic du Midi, was it horribly wrong? Would a brother and sister do that? Or a boyfriend and girlfriend?'

'I know it wasn't wrong and so do you really, we only looked at each other. I think you are supposed to be sixteen before you can say yes to having sex; but we didn't have sex did we? But I don't feel it's something I want to tell Mum and Dad about.'

'I've never told anyone else my step-Dad is not my real Dad and I don't want your Mum and Dad to know either. Promise?'

'Yes, of course.'

She told me that she had been seven when her Mum and Dad had got married. Before then it had just been her living with her Mum, who worked from home so she could look after her. Aged ten, she'd asked her Mum who her real Dad was and she had said she didn't know. She had gone to a party one night and there was too much for everyone to drink and probably someone had thought it fun to put some drugs in the drink. Her Mum woke up in bed with three boys and none of them had any idea what had happened. Nine months later Poppy was born.

This was an amazing story, just right for my book but it was private and I'd promised. Still, it was like a mystery story: who is Poppy's Dad?

We were going back to England the day after tomorrow, so we really needed to talk to Mum and Dad about Poppy. I thought it might help if it were me that introduced the subject.

'Mum, what will happen to Poppy when we go back to England? Can she always live with us? I think she might like that if her Dad doesn't mind.'

Mum wanted to talk to Poppy alone and told me to go and play with Philippe for a bit. Poppy told me all about it when we went to bed in the Blue Room that night.

'She said she would really like me to be part of her family: she had always wanted a couple of kids and a girl like me would be a perfect daughter for her and sister for you. But she was worried about my Dad, life must be horrible for him, he has lost his wife and wouldn't want to lose his daughter too, even though it would be difficult to look after me and keep his job at the same time.'

The decision was that my Mum and Dad would have a serious talk with Poppy's Dad as soon as we got back to England and try to decide what would be best for everyone.'

The journey back home was so different from the way down, Poppy and I were real friends now and had lots we wanted to talk about, only mostly we couldn't with Mum and Dad in the front seats. We were still looking for an Estonian Euro but our hearts weren't in it. We wanted to be back on the Juniper Rock where we were at home and could talk all day in private. We weren't going home, just going back to school.

Poppy was going to stay with us for a couple more days until the talk with her Dad had sorted things out and a way had been found for her to be looked after while her Dad was at work all day.

I don't know what Mum and Dad said to Poppy's Dad but they told us all about the decision as soon as they got home. Poppy's Dad was still very sad and needed to spend some time in hospital for depression. With treatment he'd be able to keep his job but he would need to get back to work fairly soon and work hard. Please would we have Poppy living with us? He'd give us some money to pay for her food and she could come and visit him whenever she liked.

Poppy was still worried about her Dad but happy about everything else and the rest of us were just happy.

Mum said she had always wanted a daughter but had never been able to have another baby. Dad looked as though he were a bit in love with his daughter already. Poppy was having her own room just across the passage from mine, the only thing was, did I want her as a sister? OK, all the boys with sisters talked about seeing them in the bath but I didn't have to look through keyholes, she'd wanted a shower together and taught me all sorts of things. Sisters don't do that. Poppy never seemed happier than when we were just lying in the sun somewhere talking about ideas and places and books we might write. Do sisters do that? They might, when they had a boyfriend, but not with a brother. I didn't want a sister, Poppy was much better.

Poppy and I knew her Dad was only her step-Dad. No one else did, until one day my Dad went to see Poppy's Dad in hospital and he told him the whole story. I overheard him talking to Mum about it and worrying about what to say to Poppy. Next day, after school, I asked her to come down the road and see the sheep with me. We hadn't done that for ages. I told her that Mum and Dad knew but thought she and I didn't. We thought about it for a long time before we decided what to do.

After dinner Poppy said 'Mum?' (she used to call them by their first names but now she felt like their daughter):

'Mum – did you know my real Mum told me my Dad was really my step-Dad? She didn't even know who my real Dad is.'

'Yes' she replied. 'It doesn't make any difference does it, you still love your step-Dad don't you?'

Dad was sitting there looking most odd, he sometimes went red and looked as though he needed to tell someone he'd just run over their cat.

'I've got something to tell you Poppy, you see I think I might be your real Dad. I was away from home, for a meeting in London, two or three months before Moth was born. I went to the same party as your Mum and I was one of the lads she woke up with in bed. Neither of us knew what, if anything, we had done.'

This was incredible news and really bad. Poppy might be my real sister. End of all happiness.

Until now each meal time seemed to involve talking about how we should sort ourselves out into a real family. Mum and Dad had wanted to adopt Poppy so she was a proper daughter for them if her Dad agreed but if my Dad were Poppy's real Dad it would all be easy. Her Mum was dead, she only had one parent, they wouldn't need to adopt.

'We'll have to get a DNA test, then we'll know for certain if I'm her Father. You two can have one too if you like because even half-brothers and sisters share quite a lot of genes.'

So one day we went off to a laboratory in Cambridge and they took some swabs from inside our mouths.

The results came two days later: Poppy wasn't Dad's child but I was. Joy, she's not my sister.

But they went back to the adoption idea and that was almost as bad. Poppy would be my legal sister even though not my biological one. Would I still be able to marry her one day? I'd never quite admitted to myself before that that was what I wanted. At least I wanted to have the chance.

I took Poppy for another trip to see the sheep and explained about not wanting a sister without actually saying I wanted a girlfriend. She soon saw what I really meant and said that she liked me more as a boyfriend than a brother.

'Don't worry, Moth, I've got a plan and I'm sure it will work.'

It did too, she told Dad that she didn't really want to be adopted.

'I hope one day I'll find my real father and if I do I don't want to be someone else's daughter. You and Mum are registered as my guardians now and that seems to work just like you are my own Mum and Dad. Can't we go on like that?'

It worked a treat, they agreed straight away.

It was getting near the end of term now and then it would be Christmas. Poppy asked me what we did for the school holiday – could we go to France again?

'I don't know, it depends if Mum and Dad think they can afford it. In good years we go there skiing and that's really brilliant. If you ask Dad he might say yes, he still wants to think you're his long lost daughter.'

He did say yes and we started planning furiously just so we could look forward to it properly. We set up Google Earth again and found our cottage. Then I scrolled it over to show her the high Pyrénées where our nearest ski station was.

'Have you got some spare skis for me? I've no idea how to use them though.'

'We haven't got skis for anyone, we rent them so we get ones that are the right size each time. Skis don't grow like you do. You can get some that are made to go slower than usual, so learners can use them more easily. You'll love it.'

We were on the school bus for the last time that year and everyone was talking about the holidays..

'Are you staying here for Christmas, Poppy?'

'No, I'm going home.'

Some people looked surprised but I remembered the Juniper Rock and knew just what she meant.

Chapter 8 – Home from home

Of course it gets dark early in December and neither Mum nor Dad like driving at night on long journeys through France. We stopped half-way home (we both want to think of France as "Home" now) and found a hotel none of us had stayed in before. Two rooms between us, dinner and breakfast. The young lady who brought the dinner menu spoke some English and obviously wanted to practice her skills.

'Would you like a kangaroo?'

Her English must be awful, she can't have meant that! But she did, there was a good choice for dinner but one of them was roast kangaroo with a range of vegetables. We all thought we'd try something new.

'Où vous les attrappez?' I joked with the waitress and she said 'In the freezer, sir.'

Kangaroo is really very good.

Upstairs we unpacked our things and got ready for bed.

'Does kangaroo make you feel bouncy at all?'

'I'm sorry Moth, I think I've been unbounced, like they tried to do to Tigger.'

I thought I might know what the problem was and said 'Good night Tigger.'

She took a long time in the shower-room and went straight to bed.

At breakfast the kangaroo girl wasn't there and an older lady gave us the breakfast menu. She didn't speak any English and the two Americans at the next table were having problems knowing what to choose. We helped translate and they seemed not to be able to cope with the idea that stewed apple and yoghurt went well together at breakfast. In the end they got fried eggs sunny-side up, even though they weren't on the menu.

'It makes you feel properly French doesn't it' said Poppy afterwards 'when you can help the foreign visitors but know that what you want for breakfast is just the same as any Frenchman would choose?'

We made good time for the rest of the journey and there was plenty of afternoon left when we got to the cottage. Mum thought I should have the Red Room with its really ancient single bed and leave Poppy in the Blue Room that we had always shared before. I asked her, as we unpacked, whether she was still feeling unbounced and she said she was a bit.

We did all the usual things, even Poppy felt they were usual, just part of the normal life there. It was Saturday tomorrow so we made long lists of stuff to buy fof Christmas and tried to work out who in the village would be coming to dinner with us. 'It'll be all of them, some time or other' said Mum and carried on making her lists.

Mum and Dad would do most of the food shopping and I wanted to sneak off to the end of the market where the gift stalls were. I needed presents for

Mum and Dad but especially Poppy. She probably wanted to make similar purchases but she would have to choose on her own. She knew enough French to get by but I did ask her if she had enough Euros.

'Yes thanks, Moth. My step-Dad gave me some Christmas money before we left England.'

I chose her present first. A whole lot of the donkey-milk soap and a really pretty little basket to put it in. Then I found a weird little snake toy made of furry cloth and I bought that too. I got Dad one of those very French folding knives, sharp with serrated edges but you use them just like an ordinary knife at dinner-time. Some French people bring their own knife like that when they come and dine with you. They keep it for every course.

It seemed a bit obvious to get something for the kitchen for Mum but there was a lovely stall run by some Arabs with a huge range of brightly coloured spices that you could measure out and have put into little glass jars. I got eight, with as many different coloured spices as I could. I remembered just in time to make a note of what they were all called.

When we got back home and got out some lunch I suddenly realised there was something wrong. It was sunny and quite warm. So warm, we put the picnic table out in the garden and had our sandwiches and wine there. Well actually Poppy and I had cidre doux, like very slightly alcoholic apple juice but fizzy and nicer. While we were drinking it, a Red Admiral flew by and tried to settle on Poppy's cider glass. It was beautiful weather, two days before Christmas, but not a good sign for the ski slopes.

Philippe, Emilie and their parents were going to spend Christmas with one of their grandmothers. They'd be here just after Christmas, would join us for skiing and had invited us to their New Year party which is always great fun.

We checked on our local ski station's website and it said that only two of the slopes were open yet and they were using snow machines to keep them going. At least the nursery slope was open, so Poppy could start to learn and we all went up there next day. There were several little shops where you could rent skis and sticks and we were soon kitted out; we had to pay just for the one day but they said if we were coming back over Christmas they would keep a note of our sizes and everything would be quicker and a bit cheaper next time.

I took Poppy up to the nursery slope. Nursery slope was a jolly good name for it, most of the kids were about six or seven and there was even a three-year-old zooming down the slope on very short skis andwith a dummy in his mouth. The ski instructor looked only a few years older than me and cheered up a lot when he saw his new pupil. I wondered whether I should stay and join his class too but decided to risk leaving Poppy and going up the ski-tow and down the green slope like Mum and Dad were doing. I knew I could do it better than them and hoped they'd soon have the blue slope open.

After three descents I skied back across to the nursery where Poppy was taking a long time being taught how to do snow-ploughs. The instructor had handed the little ones, including the boy with a dummy, to a lady instructor. I thought Poppy only needed one more day in the nursery, then I could teach her how to use the proper slopes.

Christmas came, it was still quite warm but it started to snow, snow which turned to water as soon as it hit the window. We hoped it would be better snow up on the ski slopes. So Christmas dinner was indoors, just us – Étienne and Christianne were coming round in the evening.

Dinner was chicken.

'Oh good, élevée en liberté,' said Poppy 'it had a nice life before they killed it.'

Mum had used some of the spices she had opened after breakfast and had seemed very pleased with them. Dad found his new knife was really easy to use – but it wasn't a tough chicken anyway. Poppy had kissed me when she opened her present but hadn't said much about it since.

I'd been really pleased with my presents, Mum and Dad had got me a big French book that had coloured photos and descriptions or every kind of moth in France. It was exactly the same design as one of my English moth books but it had lots of extra species that don't live in England.

Poppy gave me several sets of the special insect pill-boxes like Peter uses. He had told her where to buy them online before we left England. 'Sorry, your present won't be much use till Spring' but I reassured her 'I'll catch you some December Moths and some Winter Moths as soon as we get a still, cloudy night.'

When Dad and Mum were dozing after dinner she snuggled up a bit and said 'The basket's lovely Moth and I shall think about you every time I'm lying in the bath surrounded by asses milk bubbles. But what's the little snake for – it looks like a willy. Am I supposed to play with it?'

'I thought you knew your history, Cleopatra. It's an asp and you mustn't use it.' 'I hope I don't have to Mark Antony.'

I wasn't sure if she'd got that right, I'm not much good at Shakespeare plays and when I saw the old film I was too busy laughing at Kenneth Williams to remember who Cleopatra's lovers were.

We didn't go skiing every day, only about two or three times a week. Philippe and Emilie were back and came too, with their parents, most days. Most of the ski runs were open now and Poppy was just as happy on the green and blue runs as I was. Of course, Philippe could do red and black slopes easily and seemed determined to get Poppy to try the exciting runs with him. I was worried about this and not just because she might break a leg.

I had a quiet word with Philippe and he said 'But she's your sister and we're old friends. I like her, what's the problem?'

When he knew, he was very good, friendly to Poppy but became more interested in one of the other girls on the slopes.

New Year's Eve is a big thing in France. Philippe and Emilie's parents had invited everyone to dinner and midnight celebrations. Even though I feel French now, there are a few things I can't get used to. One of them is oysters. The supermarkets are full of them on New Year's Eve and everyone buys some for the big meal. We had loads and they're horrid. The poor things are still alive and sprinkled with lemon juice that must sting horribly. It's very hard not to think about that when your trying to swallow one and not be sick. Poppy and I managed two each and thought that was enough to be polite. Somebody said we should eat a dozen if we wanted a really good time and winked at us.

After that, the meal looked up a lot and so did the drinks. We were both allowed a little of each sort of wine, including the champagne we had at midnight. Everyone was chatting and joking and Poppy said afterwards that even she could join in without thinking about it.

'You mustn't try to think what you want to say in English, then find the right words in French, then say them, that's much too hard. I think it was the wine made me less self-conscious. I just said things in French without thinking in English. If I didn't think about it the words came out right, I even got "le" and "la" right most of the time. I think this is a new year and I'm a new person, a French one, and I don't want to be sent back to England and to school.'

I knew just how she felt, but school it was and back to England for all of us.

We all felt the same on the way back to England. It was as though we were deportees being sent off to work in the salt-mines in some far-off foreign land. Mum and Dad didn't say it quite like that but you could tell what they were thinking.

Dad asked 'Do you think it's time for a change love? Could we start a new life in France?'

'But what would you do, I can carry on working a bit from home as long as the Internet stays good out here but we need you to earn some money too.' 'I've been thinking about that, one of my friends from college days lives out here now. He makes a reasonable living being booked by big companies and government offices to do two-way translations when they have meetings with American or English companies. You don't get work five days a week but the money's good when it comes and you can be half-retired and still be as well-off as you are in England.'

This sounded really promising and over the next few weeks Poppy and I would hear bits of talk about how much the English house was worth and how long a period of notice you needed to give at school and whether Poppy's step-Dad would mind about her being exported to France with a healthy young lad of her own age.

They must have sorted that out to his satisfaction, and the school's, and the estate agent's, because one day they told us both that we'd be moving to France, for ever, from the end of the summer term.

Chapter 9 – Baby Powder

I was already thirteen and Poppy would be in a few weeks. She had been part of my family for a year and now we were moving to France: a new world, new school, new language and new friends. People seemed to expect us to mope around a bit, visiting all our old friends and favourite places and saying we'd be back for holidays and wouldn't lose touch. How wrong could they be! We spent our time upstairs on our computers, watching the French news on the internet, reading the local paper for our market town and talking to each other in French. We were going home and were going to be ready for it.

Dad sold our English car as well as the house. He'd always had a bank account with Crédit Agricole as well as his English bank, so the financial arrangements were easy. Everything we didn't want was sold or put on Freecycle and what we did want went to France in a lorry, while we travelled down by Ryanair and a rented car. In France Dad bought a Yeti: a bit like a cheap Land Rover and very practical for the roads and tracks around our new home.

It was quite a while before Dad started getting much work. Meanwhile he dug a big vegetable garden and had some chickens in a great big pen. 'Almost élévée en libertée' claimed Poppy.

Poppy and I had plenty of time before school started, French schools have slightly longer holidays than English ones and "la rentrée" would not be for five weeks yet.

'What shall we do with ourselves' asked Poppy.

'Well I know what I'm going to do – try to make a moth-trap.'

'In that case, I shall sit out here in the sun and read some of those books Mum and Dad have got about the history of this département. I couldn't do it before because the French was too hard.'

The moth trap wasn't really a trap. I'd got an old sheet off Mum and fixed the corners so you could use tent-pegs to hold the sheet spread out and firm on the ground. Then I got the most powerful lamp I could find in Mr Bricolage, one of those that people put on the gates of their big houses and light up to scare the burglars away. I could hang the light on the house wall and have it shining on the sheet. It worked a treat but you had to stay up with a net, not just wait for morning. It was like using Peter's trap that night I first met Poppy. It had been fun then too, but now I got over fifty different sorts of moth on the first night and even Poppy was impressed with how beautiful some of them were.

'Why on Earth is that one called an Elephant Hawk? It's pink and green and lovely, not a bit like an elephant.'

'It's because some people thought the caterpillars looked like an elephant's trunk. They swing their heads from side to side like a zoo elephant reaching for a bun. But most people who find the caterpillars think they are snakes. They've got eye-markings behind their heads and they swell up their front ends and look just like a mini-cobra. I think birds make the same mistake as people and that helps the caterpillars avoid being eaten.'

'I think you'd better be a biology teacher. Do all moths have interesting names?'

'Some are a bit boring "Clouded Drab" for example. But lots are really pretty: there's even a "Maiden's Blush" and a "True-lover's Knot".'

'You're just winding me up – I thought most of the people who wrote the old moth books were doctors and vicars. Why couldn't they have given such nice names to a girl's bits as they did to their moths?'

'Perhaps the vicars had never seen a girl and doctors have always used long Latin or Greek names to impress their patients.'

'I'll have to choose some names myself then.'

'Go on then, take my English moth book and you can choose some names. Here's a good one "Bloomer's Rivulet" or what about simply "Puss"?'

She laughed and ran away a bit, before sitting down and waiting for me to join her. I don't think this maiden blushes too easily.

*

When first we came here we were tourists. We wanted to go down caves, climb mountains and visit the stars. When you're at home it's different. You're part of the valley and the valley is part of you. The days aren't very different but you don't mind, you're busy just being alive. Of course we went on walks, long walks, visiting the other hamlets and finding out which were still alive. Some had one or two farming families like Étienne's. Some, two or three well-maintained empty houses that were visited most weekends by their owners. Some were deserted and sad.

One hamlet had a house where the roof was falling in but inside someone had started to put good wood-panelling on the walls. There was a table with a saucepan and a baby's feeding bottle with a perished teat. There was just one baby's sock on the table. We called it the "one-legged baby house" and wondered where he was and what he was doing now, if he were still alive.

Another of the hamlets had two big lavoirs, concrete water troughs, that were filled by a water channel and which used to be the village laundry. Ours is full of tadpoles but one of these had a big fish swimming in it. There was an old lady dressed in black, smoking a cigarette as she sat in front of her door. She said her son was up in the woods cutting poles to make sheep hurdles. She started to tell us all about what is was like when she young but she wanted to use the language she loved from when she was a girl. Patois: it sounded like Spanish and we could understand a few of the words but we never found out much about her life.

We didn't spend everyday in the valley. Mum and Dad still took the odd day off work and we all went off for a treat. One day we went right over to close by the Niaux cave to visit the biggest talcum mine in Europe.

'I didn't know talcum powder came from a mine' said Poppy. 'Do they use all that stuff just to powder babies' bottoms?'

Dad explained 'What they mine is talc – the softest rock there is. Most of it is used for things other than making powder. It's needed for making rubber and some sorts of paper for example.'

Tomorrow was Poppy's thirteenth birthday and she had chosen a much closer location for her treat than she had last year. Every year there is an international folk-dance festival in our market town, there are folk-dancing groups from all over Europe. The visiting groups were brilliant but even better were the local dancers who started and ended the whole festival and were always the favourites. They danced in traditional costumes with bizarre wooden clogs that had long, curved points. There was a children's group as well where most of the performers were even younger than us but very, very good.

Folk-dancing wasn't the only festival on that day: there was a concert in the evening that Mum and Dad really wanted to enjoy. We said we wouldn't mind if they went, Poppy had already had her treat and we'd be happy at home for the evening. They said we could choose any film we liked, off Netflix, as a thank you for letting them have a treat of their own.

'Any idea what film we'd like, Poppy?'

'No, I'm not really in the mood for a film. I think I want a shower first anyway.'

'Remember our shower? It seems a long time ago but I can remember it all.'

'Let's try again and see if it's just as much fun.'

So we did and it was.

Her breasts had got a bit bigger but they were still sort-of pointed and not like blown-up balloons. I soaped them and smoothed them.

'You've got lovely breasts Poppy.'

'Thank you for calling them that, the boys at school always say boobs if they're too big or tits if they're too small. I prefer breasts.'

'I prefer *your* breasts.'

'I wonder what the boys at our new French school will call them?'

'I know that already, assuming they use the same slang as at Philippe's school. Tits are "les tétons" while big ones are "air bags".'

'In English?'

'Yes.'

'Weird.'

We were lying on my bed and were still a bit damp from our shower.

'Stay there, I just want to show you what my parents used to do when I was little. It felt lovely.'

I got the big pot of talcum powder from the bathroom and started sprinkling it across her front.

'Did you get that when we visited the mine?'

'No, it's been here ever since I was a little kid: we don't use it often. Turn over, I'll do your back first.'

I sprinkled on plenty of talc then used my hands as softly as Mum had done when I was a kid. Poppy just lay there.

'Can I turn over now?'

I sprinkled the rest of her and spent a lot of time making sure her breasts were dry. Her nipples were lovely and hard. Then I did the rest of her, all of her.

'I'll do you now' and she did. It was bliss.

We were sitting up now and looking at each other.

'Talcum powder's lovely, babies are lucky. They get breasts as well – I wonder what that's like?'

'Try if you like.'

'Won't it hurt? Babies don't have teeth.'

'Well don't bite then.'

I didn't, I just used the tip of my tongue to feel the tip of her breast and then down beside it where I could feel a little ball of hardness behind. I let my mouth close round her nipple and started to suck gently. She sighed contentedly. There wasn't any milk of course but there seemed to be a little taste of something that made you feel happier. When I had switched to her other breast and found it was just as nice, I rolled over and lay beside her, smiling.

'That was lovely for me too, Moth. I hope my babies will be as gentle as you.'

We must have been lying there together for ages, touching each other sometimes but not saying anything more. Suddenly we heard the car draw up on the drive. Poppy moved quickly and was back in her own room putting on pyjamas. I wasn't going to wear my pyjamas. Lying in bed naked I could still smell the talcum and Poppy's hair that had left a softer, gentler smell. And I didn't think I was imagining it, there was still the faint taste on my tongue. "Happiness milk" I'll call it.

Mum was coming up stairs and went to the bathroom. She started to run her bath then, about a quarter of an hour later, called out to Dad 'Have you seen the talcum powder, love.'

He hadn't. I put it back next day. Why did she want talcum powder all of a sudden?

Chapter 10 – The Green Field

When school started it was surprisingly similar to England. I'd gone to a French primary school for a year but that is no preparation for secondary school any more than it is in England. We had to get a lift from Mum or Dad down the hill to the village, then a minibus picked us up and collected eight of us from the scattered hamlets in this valley and the next. At school we had classes and subjects and playtimes and dinners and tests and exams to prepare for. I don't need to say much more do I? The dinners were much better than in England though.

Of course we met lots of new kids in the playground and we soon ended up speaking just like them and not like the French you heard on the television or which Dad spoke so well. One of Mum's friends from Paris came to visit and asked her whether she had adopted us locally. I think she was joking but maybe she wasn't.

It was Saturday and pouring with rain. We had homework to do when Mum asked if we wanted to go into town with her.

'No thanks, you'll be in Intermarché all the time, the market will have finished. We'll stay home and do our homework.'

'OK loves.'

Upstairs, Poppy wanted to know what homework we had to do.

'Let's leave the homework and start work on that book we were going to write.'

'I thought you were going to write it?'

'It'll be much more fun if we do it together and we can help each other remember what we did and what everything felt like.'

'Will we put in everything?'

'Yes, this is only for us, we can decide what bits to leave-out or change if we ever want to show it to someone else.'

'It won't all be fun will it, remembering? What about my Mum?'

'You said once that remembering helps keep people alive – don't you want to remember her?'

'Yes I do, just as much as I want to remember the Juniper Rock and the Shower-bath and everything with you in France.'

'Which shower-bath was that then?'

'Shut-up.'

It was surprising how long to takes to write a book, even though you know all the story before you start. All you have to do is type it out on the laptop, do the spell-check and there it is. Only it isn't, you need to keep reading it and changing it until it doesn't just say what happened but what it felt like when it happened. You need some funny bits but to leave the sad or melancholy bits in too. It took us six-weeks of weekends before we thought it was done and we printed off two copies, put each in a folder, and took them to our own rooms to read and live a part of our lives again.

'Is it good enough to publish, Moth?'

'Do you want it to be? Isn't it just for us to enjoy?'

'I think I would like reading it even if it were someone else's story. And it is someone else's story, you've changed all our names and haven't said where our private homes and places are.'

'I think it's our story and our story isn't finished yet. Let's keep it for us and add to it whenever something happens worth adding. Maybe we can try and publish it when we think it's finished.'

So that's what we decided to do.

*

We were home, really home, where we would live for ever. Right now we were lying down beside each other up on the Juniper Rock.

Thinking about distant history Poppy said" 'This is our magic place isn't it. Just think about what happened in the valley down there 12,000 years ago: those 480-times Great Grandads coming here to hunt bison. They might have even got a mammoth but they never painted one.'

I replied 'There are lots of mammoth paintings in other caves a bit north of here, Poppy. We can go and see one when we go home next.'

'This is home, we're not going back to England; well, if we do, it'll be here that's home and there that's foreign.' She went on 'By the time the Romans came, there was already a silver mine just down there and someone had a big amphora of wine in the mine and dropped it. I wonder if the real relatives of Asterix tried to kick the Romans out of the valley?'

'I expect they did, like Boudicca tried to chuck them out of some foreign country up north where we lived once upon a time.'

'There's been an awful lot of fighting, the Black Prince and the French with Gaston Phoebus changing sides all the time. And all the French Catholics I've read about, burning those people who worshipped our God in a different way when they weren't going off to the Bible lands to kill people who worshipped a different God. It's horrid.'

'I think that happened even before the Black Prince's time.'

'It's still horrid and it still goes on. Just up the valley is a memorial to the maquisards who, during the last war,, when they weren't ambushing the Germans and killing them, helped people escape into Spain.'

Poppy continued 'Wasn't our escape to Spain great? Looking down from Aslan's land into the magic country below us. I really wanted to believe in Aslan, even though I knew it was all a story.'

'Poppy, do you remember one of the other Narnia stories, where Aslan tells some of the children they're getting too old and won't come to Narnia again? He says they'll have to go back to England and get jobs in the bank and look for him in disguise at church on Sundays. Where's the magic in that?'

'Do you think that will happen to us?'

'It might, we used to be able to do what we liked but it's getting difficult now. We're grown-up enough to have babies and mustn't take risks doing...well you know doing what.'

'Baiser' she said.

'Yes, the French say "baiser" and you have to guess whether they mean just "kiss" or something more. I think it's a bit rude when it means something more.'

'I like that, it's a nice word, not like "fuck", and you can still do it if you know when to stop.'

After a bit she went on: 'I suppose we are both grown-up now. I started my periods ages ago, like Mummy told me I would.'

'I guessed, you're unbounced sometimes, like the night after the kangaroo.'

'Yes, that was my first time. Mummy didn't tell me about boys: what's happening to you?'

'Wet dreams.'

'What on earth are they?'

'Well they start off nice, you dream about a beautiful naked girl who is lying there in the field beside you.'

'Is that me?'

'Yes, always. Then it all goes wrong and you wake up with a horrid sticky mess on the sheets. I was so embarrassed the first time it happened, that I tried to wash the sheet in the bathroom basin. Dad caught me and told me not to worry. He said it had happened to him and it happens to all the boys of my age. He said Mum would understand and not mind about the sheets. He thought it was just a way nature uses to get boys ready to have children but he told me not to get ready too soon, he's seen me looking at you and he would rather we went to university without having a kid to look after when we do.'

'So the magic times are fading away. I wonder what Aslan has got planned for us next? He always says in the books that he only tells anyone their own story.'

'Why are you thinking about Aslan so much when you don't believe in God? Aslan is only Jesus made friendly for kids.'

'Because I still want to be a kid I suppose. And I sometimes think some of the Bible stories are not as silly as the theories the astronomers keep making up. If there is someone out there who has already decided what I will do with my life then all I've got to do is lie back and enjoy it. No decisions, no getting it all wrong.'

'So you want to stay a kid all your life? Like Peter Pan?' 'Well, I want an awfully big adventure – but not if it involves dying, like the one Peter Pan had in mind.'

She went on 'The first part of our adventure has already been written. Perhaps Aslan knows how it will all end?'

'This is getting sillier than your astronomer's theories. Let's go further up the hill and see if we can find the mine which you can still get into.'

'And play at being children for a bit longer?' 'If you like.'

Two days later Poppy asked if we could go off and have a picnic in the Green Field. You can see the Green Field from the window of the Blue Bedroom which Poppy and I used to share. I'd called it that when I was about six because the field was a normal bright green colour but is was surrounded by sombre green trees and looked so different from a normal field.

She seemed quite well prepared, a picnic in a basket and a big picnic rug in case the ground was prickly. There weren't usually any cows in the Green Field and it was completely empty today. Some butterflies were flying over the long grass: Marbled Whites, ordinary French ones, not like those we'd seen in Narnia.

'Moth, I've been thinking about your dreams. Do you think it would work if we had our dreams together? I think I might like that. How do your dreams start?'

'I told you, seeing you lying naked in a field and feeling all happy and excited.'

'Well I'd better take my clothes off then; or you can do that if you like.'

Well, I did like and I did it really slowly and folded her clothes as I went, so I could enjoy the moments longer.

'It's my turn now.' And she started to undo my buttons. 'Isn't it big? Nearly as big as my asp. Can I see what it feels like?'

She could, and she did, and then asked if I wanted to borrow a hanky.

We both lay there, looking up at the sky and watching the butterflies.

'Do you want to see what I feel like too?'

I sat up slowly and turned towards her. I'd touched her there once before, so I thought I knew what to do. I gently parted her lips and stroked her girl's willy.

'I know what its name is now, the girls at school call it "le bouton d'amour" – the love button. Isn't that sweet?'

I hadn't looked last time, just felt, but this time I could see other bits I knew nothing about.

'I don't know nice French names for the other bits. Go down a bit.'

'Like this?'

'Yes, you can put your finger inside me if you like.'

So I gently pushed it in. 'Move it about a bit, I do that myself sometimes and it's nice.'

Suddenly, her body was moving and trying to pull my finger further in. Poppy was sighing and smiling.

Half an hour later we were still lying there holding hands.

'See, it's not the end of childhood. We can always do that and not get stuck with babies.'

Another half hour and she said 'What about those capotes anglaises things the boys talk about at school? Can't you get some of them so we could do other things safely?'

It wasn't quite the time to give her a language lesson, interesting though it is that that's what we call them in France but in England they are French letters.

'My Dad warned me about those, he says they sometimes burst and then the girl's in trouble.'

'I wonder how he knows?'

I didn't reply and after a few minutes she asked 'Do you remember when we were in Aslan's country looking at marmots and down on Narnia?'

'Of course I do.'

'Well, where did your parents go?'

'To have a picnic at a place they had visited before they were married.'

'I expect that, back then, they were just drinking wine and watching marmots don't you? Or do you think it might have been about nine months before you were born? They said it was in the Spring.'

'So we both came along a bit too early didn't we, Poppy? Would we have been very different people if our parents had waited until they were married?'

'Of course we would, I'd have had a different Dad for a start. And we'd each be as different as our own brother or sister would be if we had one now. So we wouldn't really exist at all.'

'Well, thank goodness Aslan burst that thing and put something in your Mum's wine, I don't want to be without you and I don't want to be without me.'

Poppy's thoughts drifted back to Narnia: 'Are we just joking about Aslan, or do you think someone really does know our stories in advance and writes the script?'

'I ought to say we are joking. Remember when we did Brownian motion at school? All those little specks dancing about at random because they were being hit by random molecules we'll never even see? A scientist ought to say the universe is all random just like that and I'm afraid the scientist would be right, though I'd like him not to be. The scriptwriter would have to be like Aslan, who doesn't seem to quite have full control of the story, his actors have to make decisions themselves, take risks, fight battles and hope good triumphs over evil in the end. If he were a proper God, he'd just wriggle his whiskers and the white witch would vanish. He'd keep all his characters well fed and more or less happy, like chickens in a pen waiting to go to Heaven and Tescos.'

'I don't think I ever believed in God and now I don't even want to. Aslan might be alright though, what did you say "élévée en libertée" meant?'

Chapter 11 – Learning to be Cavemen

It was almost exactly two years since Poppy's birthday visit to the Pic du Midi and one since we'd used the baby powder. I wondered if she would make the treat for her fourteenth birthday as exciting. At the time it seemed the answer was no, certainly nothng like the Green Field had been a few months ago.

Poppy wanted to go to Montsegur – it's a ruined but impressive castle on the top of a steep hill called a "pog". What fascinated Poppy was the terrible event she had read about that had happened there in 1244. The Cathars, who believed in God but not exactly what the Pope said Christians should believe in, were camped in the castle and besieged by a Catholic army. The Cathars finally admitted defeat and were given the choice of converting to Catholicism or dying. Over 240 staunch Cathars had stuck with their faith and been burnt alive in a huge bonfire.

Even though Poppy is pretty certain God does not exist, she still wanted to know all about the differences between what Cathars believed and the Catholic faith. She thought the Cathar religion sounded much more sensible but I didn't much like the idea of having to be a vegetarian.

Poppy bought a book that told all about the Cathars who had lived in the village of Montaillou. She discovered that you would only have had to be a vegetarian if you were a Cathar priest. The book had originally been written over 700 years ago by the inquisitor who had brought Cathars before the courts and recorded all they told about their lives and faith.

Poppy said 'It's almost as good as being able to talk to those people and learn all about their lives. I wish the people who painted the cave at Niaux could tell as much but there was no one to ask them and write it all down.'

I read the book too and had to admit that parts of it were as good as a novel. I'm ashamed to admit that I read the "Body language and sex" chapter first. One bit particularly stuck in my mind "People did not shave, or even wash, often......On the other hand there was a good deal of de-lousing, which was an ingredient of friendship".

Now it was February and time for my fifteenth birthday treat. I thought a visit to another cave with Stone Age art would be good, it wouldn't matter what the weather did and it would please Poppy. I chose Mas d'Azil: I'd been there when I was about nine and knew it was quite different from Niaux. It has a really spectacular river and a road, running right through the cave.

There are some engravings of Stone Age animals on the walls but most of them are in parts of the cave not open to the public. What is shown to you are the places where all the stone and bone tools and beautiful bits of art carved in bone or deer antlers were excavated. The ticket for the cave also gets you into the museum in the middle of the town, so we had my birthday lunch at a restaurant and then visited the museum.

Lots of the things the cavemen had made were purely practical, such as sharp knives made with flakes of flint that would have been fixed in bone or wood handles originally. Poppy liked the needles 'They look just like big versions of our needles – except they're made from bone with an eye carved through at one end. I wonder what they made with them?' 'Clothes I expect, it was supposed to be an Ice Age then.' 'What would they have used for cotton?' Poppy is very good at asking unanswerable questions.

I was really surprised to learn that they had not invented bows and arrows. They used spears – probably wooden poles with very sharp points made of antler or bone. They also had spear-throwers that hooked on to the spears and made it possible to throw the spear further and more accurately. The spear-throwers often had beautiful carvings on the handles – a horse's head and a deer fawn were two we saw in the museum.

Perhaps the most exciting thing we saw was a book – it was expensive but Poppy and I split the cost between us with some help from Mum and Dad. It was about another group of local caves where they're were paintings, engravings, clay models of bison and even a picture of some sort of human who might have been a witch-doctor. The caves are completely closed to the public and only the most expert archaeologists are allowed in to see them. The book was the closest we were ever likely to get to seeing what the Tuc d'Audubert and Trois Frères caves are like. Poppy said 'I think I'll study archaeology at university then they might let me see all those marvellous places.'

For months, whenever we were stuck indoors by the weather, we tried to teach ourselves how to be cavemen. We had loads of information in books but it was usually easier to stick a question in Google. There was even a video of someone lighting a fire by rubbing sticks in the way cavemen may have done. The trouble was that, whenever we tried to do something like that ourselves, it proved very difficult. Cavemen didn't have to learn their skills from books or the internet.

I did eventually manage to make a spear with a nice sharp antler point. I could throw it but when I tried a spear-thrower attachment I couldn't make it work at all.

Poppy wanted to make us proper clothes. We thought about asking the local huntsmen to give us some skins from the deer they shot but realised these would need all sorts of complicated curing to make them soft and stop them going rotten. We cheated and bought some cured skins in the market. Then we couldn't make any decent bone needles and cheated again by using the biggest darning needles we could find. Finally, we didn't know whether cavemen used thin strips of skin for stitching or if they had some sort of string or cotton made from plants. We cheated again and used rather coarse garden twine.

When they were done, our costumes were not much more than knee-length sacks with arms and some baggy trousers. We didn't even know whether they should be worn with the fur-side outside or inside. We chose outside.

*

By the end of July, when Poppy's fifteenth birthday was approaching, we had tested our clothes and tools outdoors. I could sometimes get a fire started after wearing my palms raw twizzling a stick against another piece of wood. I never even tried to use my spear for real hunting. The clothes were fine for summer wear but we were pretty sure we'd soon have died of cold in an Ice Age winter. Drawing bison on rocks with sticks whose ends we had burnt to charcoal was fun.

In early August Poppy announced that she wanted to experience the Stone Age for her birthday treat. Could Mum and Dad find us somewhere near Niaux where we could spend a couple of nights camping in the entrance of a cave and using our caveman kits?

Dad had obviously put a lot of effort into the treat. He had a friend, a vet originally from England, who lived near Niaux. Because of his job he knew practically everyone in his area, especially the farmers. He knew just the place, a little farm with some dry scrubby hillside that had a sort of cave entrance that didn't go back far. He warned us that the farming family were "hippies", as the French so charmingly still call them, less interested in making a fortune than in simple farming, cultivating a bit of cannabis and enjoying a smoke. They said the cannabis was organic and so was everything else they grew.

Mum and Dad were worried and not just about the cannabis. Mum took Poppy aside for a chat and Dad invited me for a walk. We had to promise not to try the cannabis but they seemed more worried about sex than drugs. It was no good us pretending we didn't fancy each other but we both promised that, whatever we did, we wouldn't risk making a baby.

We all called at the farm and met the farmer and his wife and their son, Guillaume, who was about our age. Dad sorted out the finances with Guillaume's parents, then drove us to near our cave. They watched my three attempts at getting the fire going (successful eventually). They'd given us some chunks of wild boar meat so we didn't need to go hunting, I think we would have died of hunger before we killed anything other than one of the farmer's scrawny sheep.

Before Mum and Dad left they wanted to be sure we had our phones with us in case of emergency.

'Cavemen didn't have phones, we'll hide them at the back of the cave just in case.'

'Alright loves, just check them every few hours in case it's us who have the emergency.'

'OK – we'll be fine. Goodbye.'

We thought wild boar on its own might not be a very balanced diet and Poppy remembered the stinging nettles we had enjoyed that day we had first met in England. We went off to pick some and wondered how you could cook stinging nettles without a cooking pot. Finally we decided to cut big slots in the meat and stuff the nettles inside, so they were kept moist while the meat cooked in the fire.

Guillaume arrived carrying a basket of small mushrooms.

'Do you want some, you'll like them they're really nice' he said grinning.

'Are you sure? They don't look like ordinary mushrooms.'

'Course I'm sure – we often eat them. Look I'll eat this one raw. See, they're good.'

So we added some mushrooms to the nettles and cooked the whole lot buried in the ashes at the edge of the fire. After about an hour and a half we reckoned it would be ready and it was.

We used a tuft of grass to wipe most of the ashes off the meat then pulled the meat off the bone, found the nettles and mushrooms and ate our first cave-meal, with fingers, off a grass plate while watching the evening sky from our shelter in the cave entrance. It was delicious, especially the little mushrooms.

Poppy wanted to know what cavemen did in the evenings. 'Do you really need to ask?'

'Well they can't do that every evening. It's probably pretty much like us, stories, playing with the kids, singing, planning what to do tomorrow. Just no books to read or screens watch.'

'I bet I know one thing they enjoyed that we don't.'

'What's that?'

'De-lousing.'

I explained to her about the Montaillou book and what it had said about how friends spent a lot of time de-lousing each other.

'That was only a few hundred years ago but they were covered in lice and I bet cavemen were too.'

'Well we're not.'

'Let's pretend.'

So we did.

Poppy spent a long time searching through my hair and finger-combing it into near neatness, before announcing I was now louse free. It had been really nice, just lying there being groomed delicately and letting your thoughts wander. I started feeling pleasantly weird, as though I was not just me but part of the whole of nature. It was very difficult to explain but I tried and Poppy said she felt just the same and wasn't it nice? So it wasn't the de-lousing that made you feel that way, I hadn't started on Poppy yet.

Poppy had quite long hair and after a bit of grooming I decided it would be fun to try braiding it, African style, like some of the girls at school did. I wasn't a great hairdresser but when it was done Poppy said she liked it, at least what she could see of it (which wasn't much). She thought it might be more practical like that for a cave-women, so she kept the braids.

'Have all the lice gone?' asked Poppy.

'Well all the head lice have.'

'Isn't that the only kind? Those were the only ones I caught at primary school.'

'Me too, but there are two other kinds in my insect books. Body lice are just like head lice but lay their eggs in your clothes and then there are crab lice that children never get.'

'Why not?'

'Because they only live amongst those coarse hairs that grow on parts of your body when you're about our age.'

'Now I know why you wanted to play de-lousing. Come on then but remember what we promised Mum and Dad.'

We'd made a bed of dry bracken in the cave before we had dinner. Now we lay beside each other and discovered that neither of us had a single louse anywhere. We were still feeling oddly elated, part of each other, and the World around us, until we eventually drifted off to sleep.

Chapter 12 — Meeting the Clan

Poppy woke me up very early next morning.

'Can't you let me sleep a bit longer, Poppy?'

'No I can't; something very strange has happened, look around you.'

'It all looks normal to me, just earlier than I usually see it.'

'Well it's not normal – look at all the trees and shrubs, there aren't as many as there were yesterday and they aren't in the same places. And what's happened to the main road that goes to Toulouse? We could hear it and see it in the distance yesterday but now it's gone. I can't see or hear any of the farm cows or sheep either. What's happening, Moth?'

I could see that Poppy was scared and I was getting worried too.

'Let's get our phones and see if there is any message from Mum or Dad. If not, we can phone them.'

Poppy agreed this was a good plan but when we looked on the ledge, where we had left our phones, there was no trace of them. We were both starting to panic now.

'Who could have taken them?'

Poppy replied: 'I don't know. Let's go up to the farm, Guillaume's parents must get up early to milk the cows. We can ask to use their phone to tell Mum and Dad ours have been stolen, unless it's Guillaume playing a trick on us of course.'

But it wasn't a trick; it was much worse. When we got to where the farm had been, it wasn't there. No farmhouse, no barns, no animals, no people.

Now we were really scared. I pointed out that the only sensible thing to do was to walk about until we found a house, or a least a person, and ask for help.

Poppy agreed 'Yes, let's go downhill a bit, I think there were some farms down there or we might find the road with some traffic.'

We had been walking for almost fifteen minutes when a group of about ten animals appeared from one of the bushy areas, they were about the size of cows but weren't cows. Poppy soon realised what they were:

'They're just like the prehistoric paintings in the caves – bison! Is there a bison farm near here?'

'I've never heard of one – and look what's following the them!'

Four men dressed in clothes made of skins and carrying spears and spear-throwers had spread out and were trying to creep-up on the smallest bison.

Poppy thought 'They must be making a film.'

'I can't see any cameras – I think they might be real hunters!'

We watched. The men were good hunters. Two of them, with a couple of dogs, scared a young bison so it ran towards the other two who were in hiding. They speared the beast and immediately started cutting off its skin and rolling it up. Then they fixed the carcase on a pole that two of them carried on their shoulders and all four set off in our direction.

We had a quick whispered conversation:

'They can't be real cavemen can they? That would mean we've gone back in time and that only happens in stories. Scientists say it's almost certainly impossible. They must be re-enactors playing cavemen, like we were trying to do, or something like that. We'll have to ask them for help.'

Poppy whispered 'I hope you're right but what if the scientists are wrong and this is 10,000 BC?'

'I think we'll just have to smile and say our names. If we really have gone back to caveman time they won't speak our language so we'll need to try and be friendly and hope they will take pity on us.'

It was soon obvious they were real cavemen. As they got nearer we could see that they were just as surprised as we were. They stopped, said something we couldn't understand and then stared approvingly at Poppy. I decided it was time for introductions, I thumped my chest and said 'Moth' then Poppy just pointed her hand at herself and said 'Poppy.' They didn't respond with anything that sounded like names but chatted a bit amongst themselves. Then they looked closely at our skin clothes, feeling the joins and stitches and then burst our laughing. They obviously recognised bad workmanship when they saw it.

They did seem friendly though, especially towards Poppy, and they made it clear with signs that they wanted us to follow them. So we did.

Apart from their clothes and the language they spoke, the other very obvious thing was the smell – not the smell of the dead bison but of the cavemen. It was a mix of wood-smoke, which smelt quite nice, and unwashed human, which didn't. Poppy and I talked about it later and agreed that people who could only rarely change their clothes, kept most of them on day and night and almost never went for a swim, were bound to smell pretty bad. We wondered if we would ever be able to live close to them without being repelled by the smell.

In half an hour we saw the big porch of a large cave up on the side of the valley. We realised that it was the Niaux cave but without the car park and buildings that had been there before and set in a different kind of countryside. The cave we were making for was lower down, near the river. There was a good big fire burning in the cave entrance and maybe twenty or so people, some resting by the fire, two carving bits of bone, one feeding her baby at her breast and several kids were playing with a few dogs.

Everyone seemed very pleased to see the bison and the huntsmen, who they were clearly praising for their hunting skill. We guessed they were also hearing about finding us, they were talking and pointing at us and one of the hunters tried to say our names. He was quite good at saying 'Poppy.'

The bison skin had been unrolled and two men were scraping the bits of flesh and fat off, using sharpened stones and little knives whose blades consisted of a short row of sharp flint-flakes held in a deer antler handle.

'They must be going to make that skin into clothes' said Poppy.

'I wish they'd make some for us – ours are rubbish and they know it. If this is the Ice Age, even the end of it, we'll need some clothes like theirs.'

Their clothes were made of skins, some deer, some bison, mostly with the hair scraped off but still worn fur-side outside, skin-side inside. The main piece of clothing was a long coat with arms and a hood. It opened down the front with sort of buttons made from bits of deer antler, lower down they wore quite baggy trousers and long socks. Their boots were soft leather but with hard leather stitched on as a sole. We learned much later that this was the summer clothing, in the cold of winter they added lovely fur shirts and pants made from wolf, beaver or otter skins and worn under the bison skin coat and trousers.

We could see that they were looking at us, then at their stock of spare clothes, while they chatted a bit before agreeing what to do. They sorted out two sets of clothes that seemed likely to fit us when they held them against us. They signalled to us indicating we could put on the clothes. So we changed our home-made clothes for their professionally made new ones. They were beautifully soft leather and the front of each coat had an animal design on it, like the ones everyone else was wearing. They seemed to have been burnt into the coats' skin, we learned later it was done with glowing sticks used as paint brushes. Now we looked like everyone else in the cave but what would it be like to live with them?

Chapter 13 – Kiss-feeding and Body Odour

The sun was high-up which suggested it was near mid-day. We were feeling very hungry, so the sun was probably right and we were pleased to see people sit down near the fire and pull out some bits of meat. The bison had not been cut-up and cooked yet, this was a smaller animal and it tasted a bit like pork.

'It might be wild boar again' said Poppy.

We discovered later it was an isard, a small goat-like creature. Everyone was enjoying it, even the little kids too small to gnaw meat off the bone themselves. The adults chewed nice bits of meat for a few minutes then seemed to almost spit it into a kid's mouth.

'What a horrid way to feed a baby' I whispered to Poppy.

'You might think differently if it were your kid' she replied.

I didn't have to wait as long as Poppy predicted. I just thought about it a bit that evening.

When a baby gets to the stage where it can start eating real food, as well as getting milk from its Mum, it can't just start chewing lumps of meat off the bone like older children and adults do. The way my parents would have fed me (with little jars of mushed food or stuff prepared with a blender) is not an option for cavemen. We learnt later that they called their method "kiss-feeding" which makes it sound much nicer. Thinking about it, kiss-feeding is probably better than the blender – the kid's mother, or sometimes someone else, chews a mouthful of food until it's really soft and probably partly digested (we had done digestion at school in biology and saliva-spit starts the process).

Then the adult passes some of the chewed food straight to the youngster's mouth. Not only will digestion have started but the saliva probably has antibiotic in it that will kill some of the bugs. Maybe that's why all animals, not just us, lick their wounds. The other big advantage is that anyone with something to eat can feed one of the Clan's toddlers. Within the Clan anyone can, and does, help with the children – they are expected to and enjoy doing it. Of course the Clan members aren't strangers – they are part of a big family and think of the kids as theirs too.

When Poppy and I had been there about a week, the kids were confident enough to treat us like anyone else. A small child with lovely, long, dark eye-lashes and a charming smile would sidle up and say 'food' if it could speak, or simply point at its mouth. You'd sit the kid on your lap, while you chewed some nice food and then pass some on the tip of your tongue to the kid's open mouth.

I was really surprised at what a lovely experience this was, something I had felt so disgusting. I was really proud when a kid chose to ask me to feed it. It makes the child partly yours and you are doing something important for it and the Clan. I suspect it is a bit like the feeling a mother has when she puts her baby to the breast. Who dare I ask if I'm right?

After a few weeks our favourite kid was Albarran; he looked about three and was probably old enough not to need kiss-feeding but he still liked it and when we discovered that he was an orphan we guessed he wanted companionship as much as feeding. We spent ages with him and some evenings he would wriggle in with us, amongst the skins we used as bedclothes, near the fire.

It was only me who had initially been disgusted by the kiss-feeding but both of us had started by thinking we would never get used to the smell of the cavemen.

A couple of weeks later we knew there was no problem. By then we must have smelt the same way and didn't notice it much, except close to, when we could recognise someone in the dark by their smell almost as easily as seeing them by day. There seemed to be three components to our smell: the "Clan scent" that made us all feel like one big family and was different from the smell of the rare visitors from another clan, the "personal scent" that identified you to everyone else and a sort of "close" smell that your real friends knew and which told them, sometimes, the way you were feeling, especially the way you were feeling about them.

It's difficult to keep to things that happened on day one of our stay with the Clan without using things that happened later to help explain events. Back to our first mid-day meal. Basically it was just meat cooked in the fire. There was water in big skin bags that was poured into carved wooden cups for us to drink and a woven basket full of bilberries to finish off with.

By the end of the meal I needed a pee and could see that Poppy was feeling the same. What was the correct etiquette? We'd seen the youngest kids just going a few paces outside the cave but adults disappeared on their own and came back in a few minutes – so we guessed you had a wild-wee some decent distance from home. No one seemed surprised when we took our turn.

Later we discussed what the expected behaviour was when you needed a poo and decided to take the same approach, just a lot further from the cave. 'We can always find a stream to wash our hands afterwards' said Poppy. It wasn't long before we discovered that washing hands wasn't really necessary. Back on farms in our own time farm animals produce soft, messy turds like cow-pats and could have benefited from the sort of loo paper humans needed to use. Wild animals typically produce hard, smooth droppings that leave the animal's backside clean. The people in the Clan, and soon us too, behaved like wild animals and hands could remain unwashed but clean. We guessed it was because we were getting a more natural diet.

That's not to say the people never washed, just not that often. The stream near the cave provided our drinking water and then ran on down to the river with a path beside it giving access to the shallows and little pools. Nearest the cave, men or women could bathe together but further along was a section that only girls and women used. Poppy told me that everyone welcomed some privacy when it was what the Clan called "moon-bleed time". At other times, none of the girls minded a few lads around while they were having a normal wash.

After lunch, no one seemed especially keen to get back to work and sat around the fire chatting. Poppy and I started talking to each other in English. I suppose we were afraid they might understand French but it was soon clear they could only speak their own language and that we would need to learn it as quickly as possible.

'There seems to be quite a lot of them – lots more than just a family. I suppose they are a sort of clan' said Poppy and she continued 'Let's call their language "Clanguage" but how are we going to learn it?'

'The same way we learnt French, listening to people when we know roughly what they are talking about and getting them to help us when we know a few words and can say things like "what's that?". Let's go and play with the children, that's probably a good way to start.'

There were five children, three boys and two girls, who were old enough to be let out to play but young enough not to be expected to do much work. All the ages seemed shifted a bit compared with our World. The youngest boy was about three and would not have been allowed out on his own at home. He became our kiss-feeding friend Albarran. The eldest girl was about nine, comparing her with two young mothers nursing babies by the fire, she would probably have a baby of her own in four or five years time.

'Do you think we'll recognise their games?' asked Poppy.

We did. As soon as they were outside they were racing about playing a strenuous version of "tag" that seemed to allow you to avoid being caught if you were touching the trunk of a pine tree. When they started to get tired, they switched to "hide and seek" or tossing bits of bone like five-stones.

It was only about half-an-hour before they tired of games and settled down to what we soon realised was work. Or was it? They seemed to be really enjoying themselves. They were going hunting. In the wet grass around one of the ponds, they had soon caught about twenty frogs and put them in the leather bags that most of them carried. The frogs became part of the evening meal. Then the kids went wading into the river and picking out big shells that we eventually realised were mussels. Finally they competed with each other to see who could pick the most bilberries. It was time to take everything home and give it to whoever was doing the cooking today. Of course they got lots of praise, just like the adult huntsmen had. So cavemen, thanks to the children and their mothers, who mainly searched for plant food and tended the fire, had a good varied diet not just the great chunks of meat the huntsmen brought home.

Weeks later, when we helped the children catch lots more mussels, we made two really exciting discoveries. The first was that, when the mussels were cracked open to prepare them for eating, a few had beautiful pearls inside them. These were greatly valued by the Clan and made into lovely necklaces. Even better, while I was wading along in the river looking for mussels, I saw a small lump of shiny yellow metal. Both Poppy and I were certain it was an ingot of real gold, it was very heavy and anyway gold is about the only metal you can find in nature in its pure state. Most metals (like copper and iron) are ores that take special skills to turn into metal, skills the Clan people would not discover for thousands of years.

I showed the gold to the man who made the best pearl necklaces and he was really excited by it. I asked if he could make it into a necklace for Poppy and he said he would if I gave him half the gold to make a necklace for someone else. He heated the gold at the edge of the fire then shaped it by hitting it gently with stone implements. He made a really beautiful necklace and had included a row of pearls mixed in with the gold disks. Poppy said it was the most beautiful, and the most valuable, thing she had ever been given. Poppy was for ever taking the necklace off so she could admire the workmanship.

'You know there's something that really puzzles me about this necklace. The man who made it has obviously used gold before and I bet people find bits of gold in the river quite often. The name of the river means "gold river" in modern French but people only find it rarely now. I guess it was much more common before the Romans arrived and stole most of it. The real puzzle is that all the books about

Stone Age cave painters say they didn't use metal. But we know they use gold and since gold is fairly easy to shape and keep pretty the Clan people may have been using it for ages. Why haven't the archaeologists found any Stone Age gold items?'

I had to think about this for quite a time before I could come up with even a vaguely plausible explanation.

'Perhaps it's because the gold is so highly valued, and quite rare, that people didn't lose it where archaeologists might find it. They make thousands of spears, spear throwers, stone tools and little sculptures and lots get lost or bust and thrown away. You wouldn't do that with gold, if it broke you could shape it into a new bit of jewellery. Probably gold things got handed on from one generation to the next and by the time many gold objects were lost or buried it was into Bronze Age times. Can you think of a better theory?'

She couldn't but asked 'Can you date gold by carbon dating like you can wooden things?' I didn't know.

We'd been right about using the children to learn Clanguage. We mostly learned the names of all the different plants and animals we saw – hundreds of different words. They knew the local wildlife much better than anyone, adult or child, we'd ever met at home. They soon told us their own names: the two girls were Usoa and Neria, the boys Bittor, Benat and little Albarran. The adults still avoided using their names when we were nearby – very odd.

Chapter 14 – Children of the Gods

As soon as we joined the Clan we noticed couples sitting side by side, or lying next to each other, engrossed in grooming each other's hair and looking closely into all the body's nooks and crannies.

'You were right about de-lousing' said Poppy.

Often the couples were boy and girl or man and woman but it was common to see other pairings: two women or a child with an adult but rarely two men. They weren't at all ashamed at having lice, everyone had them, including us after a few days with the Clan.

When Poppy and I had caught head lice at primary school we were promptly shampooed with insecticide. Now we had all three types of lice.

Poppy and I were watching two Clan members (they didn't seem to mind even though they partly undressed so the louse-hunting could proceed).

Poppy said 'I know where I've seen this before – on television.'

'Really, what strange channel have you been watching?'

'Attenborough – baboons and gorillas do exactly the same, searching through each others fur, and they seem to really enjoy doing it and having it done to them.'

'It looks like cavemen enjoy it too, perhaps we should try again now we've got lice.'

'I'm itching to.' 'I'm itching too – I wonder how many lice we've got?'

Like most things that the Clan members seemed to be expert at from childhood, we needed tuition to perfect our louse-hunting technique. How to catch them then pop them by squashing them between two finger nails was the most important lesson. The other was when and where to do it: lying on all the skins beside the fire was lovely and warm, even with not much on in the way of clothing, but you couldn't do it when going to bed because there was not enough light. It was still summer-time so the other option was to wait for a warm sunny day and partly strip-off somewhere secluded in the countryside.

De-lousing is one of the best forms of courtship behaviour Poppy and I know but we had to be careful and remember our promise to Mum and Dad.

De-lousing is not just for courting couples. More or less anyone, or any child, can ask to be de-loused or ask if you would like them to de-louse you. The result was usually the same, you de-loused each other.

Most of the girls braided their hair, spending a long time helping each other to get it right. Poppy soon had my poor attempts replaced with professional braids. The boys and men just had long hair (and the men beards) often a bit tangled and that would be untangled during a de-lousing session. If a girl was being de-loused by a boy (and she usually was) her hair always got completely messed-up and she needed another session with her hair-dresser friend afterwards.

Poppy and I soon decided that it was alright for either of us to join in de-lousing with anyone who asked us. People chat while de-lousing and just to you. We had started to speak "Clanguage" and talking to people one at a time was a really good way of learning the language properly. Also it was a great way of making friends.

We eventually discovered why we knew so few people by name. Clansfolk believe that if someone knows your name then they would have power over you, so it was wise to keep your name secret until you were happy that a stranger was your friend. The children had been less wary and had let their names slip straight away but it was some weeks before we knew everyone's name. One of our new friends told us that it was because we had revealed our names on our first meeting that they had decided we were safe to take back to the cave.

A combination of learning from the children and our de-lousing friends meant that we were soon able to speak Clanguage but not very well. If whoever you are talking to tries hard, and sometimes repeats what he thinks you mean, then you get by. The really difficult thing is to understand a story. You don't know what the story is about, so you can't make any intelligent guesses as to what the storyteller means.

Most evenings, as it was getting dark, someone would tell a story or there might be singing or dancing instead.

Zadolin was the oldest of the men in the Clan and clearly the religious leader. When it was his turn to tell a story it always concerned the Gods or spirits, what we could learn from them and what they wanted us to do. This is the first story we heard from him, we didn't understand much at the first hearing but it was a popular tale and he told it often. Like the rest of the Clan, we could recite it word-perfectly eventually.

In the beginning the Sun God, Moon God, Jupiter, Saturn, Mars and Venus lived in the heavens with the stars. They carried their torches as they searched amongst the stars for something interesting to do.

Eventually they got bored and said 'there must be something more exciting than stars' and decided to take a look at the Earth.

'That'll be a waste of time' said one of the Gods 'it's dark and flat and dead and horrid.'

The others thought it was worth a try and took care to leave their huge torches circling in the sky, near Earth, so they could see where they were going. When the Sun God's torch was shining it was really bright and the Gods called that daytime. Night-time was when you had only the Moon God's torch or just the stars.

The Earth was flat, so the Gods made it more interesting by making high mountains and deep valleys.

Then they said 'It still doesn't do anything' and thought some more.

What they thought was 'Rain'. They made it rain for forty days and forty nights, really hard. The rain filled the valleys and hollows and made rivers and lakes. On the tops of the mountains the rain was snow instead of rain.

'We need some things that move about and do things, to make it really interesting' said the Gods.

So they made lots of animals: fish in the rivers, frogs in the ponds and lots of furry animals and birds all over the place.

The first thing the animals all said to the Gods was 'We are hungry, please give us something to eat' so the Gods covered the land with grass and moss and trees and lots of other plants and most of the animals had plants to eat and were content.

Some of them decided they did not like their plants and ate other animals instead and the Gods were not very pleased with them. They didn't destroy them though, they just left them alone to see what would happen and whether the animals would get it all sorted out for themselves.

Sometimes, just for fun, a God would go to live inside an animal to see what it was like and to make the animal learn to do new things.

Gods cannot have children themselves and when they saw all the animals breeding and taking over the Earth they decided they wanted children too. Gods are spirits so the only way they could make a new God was to put part of their spirit into an animal and let it live there, learning about the Earth, until the animal itself died. Then the spirit could join its relations in the spirit world of the Gods.

The Gods wanted a really good animal to raise their spirit children so they made a new kind, a clever one that could make tools and clothes and talk easily to each other and eat lots of different things. As a present the Gods gave them fire.

From that time to this the Gods have mostly kept themselves hidden from the people. But they are there and the people have slowly learned more about them. The people know that they are the children of the Gods and one day will become God spirits themselves. Meanwhile, everyone should respect and worship their ancestors who are already Gods in the spirit world.

As the first few weeks went by we began to feel at home with the Clan. We were learning the language, making some friends and getting used to the food, work and social life. In some ways it was exciting and fun but there was one thought that always spoiled the enjoyment. Would we ever get back home?

We talked about this a lot but never came to any useful conclusions.

We had no idea what had made us make the journey back in time and so we could have no idea as to what we might do to get back home. We must just wait and hope and see what happened. Meanwhile, enjoying being a member of the Clan was the only sensible thing to do.

If we did get home one day would we arrive at the same time as we had left? That would be like the Narnia stories and we hoped it would happen to us because then we would find Mum and Dad without them ever really noticing we had gone. If we spent say a year with the Clan, and then got home a year after we had left, that would be awful. Mum and Dad would have searched for their lost children for ages and eventually decided we must be dead.

We had some hope that we wouldn't get back home before we had left, if we did that then there would be two copies of each of us alive at the same time. We hoped that was impossible.

What if we never got home but spent the rest of our lives with the Clan? In some ways that wouldn't be too bad (except for Mum and Dad pining for their disappeared children). Clan life was a good society, not too hard work, plenty of friends and fun but, unlike our Clan friends, we knew what the far future held and did not believe the simple, reassuring religious beliefs that made the Clans-folk know that all would be well when they or a friend died. We would need to try and forget our past (or did we mean our future?) and try to believe in the same things the rest of the Clan did. Impossible.

If we did spend the rest of our lives with the Clan our lives would probably not be very long ones. People didn't keep exact counts of their ages but it seemed you were very lucky if you got to be fifty and most folk were dead by forty. Young children died too, of accidents or diseases.

We once tried to estimate how much of each week people spent enjoying themselves rather than working or sleeping. It was difficult because most people didn't seem to distinguish work from pleasure. They enjoyed their work and that was probably because it was so varied and pretty skilful. They did what they enjoyed doing, not what an employer said they had to do. But there was a lot of time spent on things that were entirely pleasure: singing, dancing, telling stories, playing with children and making more children. We reckoned that over a forty-year life-span a member of the Clan would spend more time on enjoyment than would most people from our time who had lived an eighty-year span.

Even more importantly, we would be living in a Clan instead of a little family. In our own time home was Mum, Dad and a couple of kids. Now we were the kids and one day would be a Mum and Dad. There might be some grandparents around sometimes but mostly they lived on their own and died lonely in a care-home. Clan life was vastly superior, like a big family where everyone was a friend and helped each other. You'd never need a baby-sitter or someone to look after your dog. You wouldn't have to work at some boring job, the same thing every day, just to get the money to live on. What you needed you would catch, find, make yourself or get a skilful friend to make for you.

Your kids wouldn't need school but would learn much more about their World and the complex skills they needed, just by being free to play and do simple tasks as well as helping grown-ups and learning from them. If you were sick or injured everyone would try their best to look after you. No one ever went hungry and had to live on the street or die imprisoned in an old folks home.

Clan life had its dangers, whatever your age, but some of these dangers are what made life fun, like hunting.

Finally, Clans-folk knew their life was a part of nature and would never change. People were quite rare and could kill all the food they needed without making a species go extinct or even get any rarer. Everything was recycled or rotted away naturally – no pollution.

People didn't get towards the end of their lives full of sadness about how the World had changed (and got worse) since their own childhood. The Clan would live in much the same world for another few thousand years, although there might be changes in the climate as the Ice Age warmed up some more but these changes would be much too slow for anyone to really notice.

We both felt that a Clan life would be a good one even if a bit short. The only real snag was that, unlike the real Clan members, we knew what was going to happen in a few thousand years and that Clan life was only a temporary garden of Eden. Once people domesticated farm animals and plants and invented iron, everything would start going wrong. People would live in much bigger groups and most would be forced to work for the rulers of the community. Worse, there would be constant wars using the new metal weapons.

But if it wasn't that we were missing Mum and Dad our choice would have been to stay with our Stone Age Clan for a few years, as long as we got home in the end.

Chapter 15 – Fitilwyn

Fitilwyn wasn't a child any more, she had just graduated from childhood to young adulthood but had not yet had a baby. I think she was about twelve – girls start having babies very early here.

At first I did not know her name of course – but she risked telling me eventually. Fitilwyn soon became my closest de-lousing companion (after Poppy of course). As soon as I could talk a bit of "Clanguage" she followed me when I went for a walk one sunny day and asked if she could de-louse me.

She was very pretty with beautifully braided hair but I would have said yes whatever she looked like because I wanted to talk to her and learn the language better.

She was very good at her job and must have squashed loads of my body and head lice before switching to searching for crotch-lice. Having delicate fingers searching your body is extremely nice, similar to the joys of talcum powder that Poppy and I had discovered together. Delicate fingers searching for crotch lice is more than just pleasant and risks being embarrassing. Fitilwyn said something at one point which I think meant 'coo look at that.'

When it was my turn to hunt Fitilwyn's lice I did an adequate job although I was still less than perfect at "search and destroy". Her breasts were beautiful and quite small, like Poppy's had been when she was twelve.

When I was about to move in on the crotch lice she said 'Not now, I've got a moon-bleed, I had my first one last month, that's why I want a baby soon.'

I walked back home with her and, when she went to join her sister and sister's baby, I went to find Poppy. She'd been off de-lousing with one of the lads and I got a bit worried about what she might let herself in for. Come to that, what was I letting myself in for?

It was only a couple of days before Fitilwyn asked me to go de-lousing again.

I said 'Alright, but I want to know what your name is first. You know mine already, everyone does.'

'It's Fitilwyn – but I've never told anyone who isn't part of our Clan before.'

'That's a really pretty name, do you know what it means?'

'It's the name of a little flower that you find in shady places in the spring. The flowers are white and the stem thin, so even a little breeze makes it blow in the wind. I'll show you one in the spring if you are still here then.'

'I think I've seen those flowers in my own country. They really are very prett: like you.'

'Thank you, Moth. Time for lice, you can look first if you like and my moon-bleed has finished.'

When it was Fitilwyn's turn to hunt she soon managed to get me over-excited and this was obvious when she started looking for crotch-lice.

She wasn't embarrassed, I don't think the Clansfolk get embarrassed much about anything. 'Will you do something for me Moth?'

'If I can, what do you want Fitilwyn?'

'A baby, will you put one inside me?'

The way I was feeling, it was very difficult not to say yes and get on with the job straight away, although I suspected I would be incapable at the moment.

I thought 'I mustn't, she's too young. And why not one of the boys from her own Clan? And what would Poppy think?'

I said 'I want to Fitilwyn, any boy would with a pretty girl like you. But I'm scared, what will the members of the Clan say? Won't they be annoyed about some stranger coming and giving one of their girls a baby? I don't know the rules in this Clan: does a boy choose a girl and stay with her for all her babies? Is it the boy or the girl or both or the girl's parents who do the choosing?'

Fitilwyn explained 'There isn't just one rule. There are lots of ways of choosing but it's not always easy.'

She paused, then said 'Sometimes a mother wants to give her daughter to one of the important men in the Clan. That's what my mother wants, to give me to her brother who has already got lots of children from three different women. I don't want him, he's a nice uncle but he's old and my mother's brother. It would be almost like your own brother putting a baby in you and that should never happen.'

She continued 'Most of the boys a bit older than me have already got sons or daughters with other girls. They'd give me a baby if I asked but they would prefer the babies they have already. The best way of getting a baby is to wait for someone from another Clan to visit. Everyone knows that a father from a different clan usually produces strong, healthy, clever children. That's why many of our young men go visiting other clans and some of them have brought their girls back here to live with us. I don't mind coming to live with your clan if you don't want to live here with us for ever. Please can I have your baby?'

This was very difficult – what an offer! But I loved Poppy and it almost felt as though we were married and I ought to be faithful to her.

I said 'I can't now, Fitilwyn. You got me so excited when you looked for lice that I spilt all my baby juice and I don't think I could give you a baby today. You know Poppy is my close friend. Well, I need to talk to her about what the rest of our Clan back home would think. If she says it's alright, I'll try.'

'Thank you Moth, will you have talked to her by tomorrow?'

'Probably.'

It was not an easy talk with Poppy. I started by asking her about how she was getting on with her de-lousing partners.

She said 'I've got five of them, two girls and three lads plus the odd kid now and again. I wanted to talk to different people so I could learn different bits of the language and find out all the rules and traditions here. The boys are the real problem, I have to admit that some of them are handsome and are very good at making de-lousing exciting but you can see they are each waiting for a signal from me that they can have a shot at making me pregnant. I've told each of them that, in the Clan I come from, girls must not have babies until their parents have met the boy and approved of him. If a girl travelling in foreign parts came home with a baby, she would be thrown out of the Clan and her baby with her.

They seem to accept that as a good enough reason but one of them was bright enough to spot the hole in my story. He said "But you always share your night-time skins with Moth and I can't believe he doesn't do some baby-making when he can."

I explained that you are part of my Clan and approved of by my parents but they had made us promise we would not start a baby until we came home. So we try to give each other pleasure but without actually making babies.'

I was very impressed with all this, Poppy had come up with a story that was mostly true and would be believed by everyone in the Clan. I told her how good her story was and then asked her views on the Fitilwyn problem.

Poppy thought for a bit before saying 'Of course it's easy for a boy, no one's going to mind much if you give a girl a baby if she wants you to. Unless you were to catch the pox from her and give it to me I suppose.'

'That won't happen, she's twelve, she's never had sex with anyone and I haven't seen any signs of disease.'

'You've looked then?'

'Of course, we de-louse each other.'

'I'm not very happy saying this but I think while we live with the Clan we should try to live as they do. You want to start hunting even though, in our World, sticking spears in wild animals would land you in court. So would getting a twelve-year old pregnant but this isn't our World, or it wasn't until a few weeks ago. Be nice to her and help her look after the baby when it comes, if we are still here then.'

'Thank you Poppy, but I would much rather it was your baby.'

'So would I but not just yet.'

'What if we never get home and live the rest of our lives here?'

'If we are still here in a year's time0, let's try for a baby then.'

Fitilwyn tracked me down next day and said 'Well?'

'Do you know a nice quiet, warm place that might be good for de-lousing?'

'Yes, I know the perfect place but I don't think I've got many lice left, you got most of them yesterday.'

'Never mind, I'm certain we'll find something to do.'

We did, and it was extremely pleasant for me but I was a bit worried about Fitilwyn, she was so young, and fairly small, that I found it a bit difficult to get inside her. When it was all over she looked pleased and happy and kissed me some more. Then she looked down between her legs and started to cry.

'What's wrong my love?'

'I'm bleeding, so that means I'm not going to have a baby. Everyone knows that.'

'It doesn't always mean that, the first time a girl lets a boy try to put a baby in her it sometimes tears her flesh a bit and she bleeds a little. It won't happen next time and it's only if you get another moon-bleed that you'll know there isn't a baby.'

She cheered up immediately. 'I hope there is a baby but can we do it more times in case there isn't? It was lovely. Thank you, Moth.'

'We can do it every few days if you like, until we know the baby is coming. The moon is full now, if we see it get small and full and small again without you having a moon-bleed, then the baby will have started to grow.'

It must have happened at one of our first attempts, Fitilwyn had no more moon-bleeds and her belly and breasts began to swell slightly. She was so happy and did not seem worried about what childbirth would be like. This was not because she didn't know what to expect, she had helped when her sister had her baby.

I asked 'Does the father come and help when his girl is having a baby? They often do in my country.'

'Do you want to? I don't think I want you to be there, it's always just your mother and other ladies who have had lots of babies themselves and know what to do, plus a sister or two if you have them. Men wouldn't like it and you might not like me any more if you had to see what happened. Why not ask to go hunting with the men instead?'

I decided to take her advice.

A few weeks into her pregnancy Fitilwyn called me over and said she wanted to give me something.

'What is it?'

'I've made it for you because you have given me a baby. Girls always make one for the father of their child, to say thank you. It's called a baby-gift.'

She unwrapped the bit of skin that was hiding it and there was a strange little carving; a very pregnant lady with large, milk-ready breasts and a head with no real detail at all apart from some cross-scratchings to represent the braided hair. I'd seen things like this in the museums in our own time; they were called Venus figurines and no one knew why they were made. Now I knew: they were to show a man that his pleasures had been put to good effect and a new member of the Clan was about to arrive.

I thanked Fitilwyn and asked if the figurine was her.

'Not really, it's just a woman expecting a baby and that's me now.'

'But where is your face, yours is a really pretty face.'

'Faces aren't important, the carving shows what is important for a new baby – good big breasts. Anyway, how do I know what my face looks like? You can see my face but I can't.'

I'd never thought of that – no mirrors.

Only a week later disaster struck: her sister's baby died and both sisters were distraught.

Fitilwyn's sister's child had fallen and cracked his head. The next morning he had died. Everyone gathered round the Clan fire and, even though it wasn't the usual time for a story, Zadolin had clearly chosen the most appropriate of his religious tales and made it personal for Pellkita and Fermin's tragedy. He was very good, like a sympathetic vicar comforting the parents of a dead child.

This is what he said:

Gilamu was Pellkita's first baby, a gift from Fermin and the Gods, a first baby to be proud of. He had seen only one summer but could walk and had just started to talk. He would have been like his father, a great hunter and clever flint-smith. But he has died. He cut his leg climbing a sharp rock, fell off the rock and hit his head. He lived only one day more.

Pellkita has cried and been comforted by Fermin but they know what must be done and doing it will help them stop crying. They must build a pile of branches near the rock that killed Gilamu and decorate it with flowers. Then they must put Gilamu's body in place and carry fire from the Clan hearth to light his pyre.

The flames will help Gilamu's spirit quickly go back to the world of the Gods that it left only a short time ago.

The Gods will welcome him back but say 'You should not have climbed that rock, you need to spend many years as a human before you are ready to live in the spirit world with us. We will let you sleep now and when you wake you will be a person again but be more careful next time.'

Pellkita and Fermin followed Zadolin's instructions and, after doing so, seemed much less sad. The Gods had promised to send Gilamu back to them.

Pellkita had still been feeding Gilamu and now he was gone her breasts hurt as well as her heart. She didn't help with feeding any of the other babies and soon her milk-flow stopped and her moon-bleeds started. She asked Fermin to help bring Gilamu back.

She didn't give Fermin a new baby-gift, it was their own baby coming back to them. Fitilwyn was delighted that the returning Gilamu would be born only a few months after her own baby.

When Fitilwyn gave birth to a boy we decided to call him Beorn because we liked the name and it was similar in both our languages. We hoped he would grow as brave and strong as a bear, which is what the name means.

I liked cuddling Beorn but there wasn't much else I could do for him while he was so young. Cave babies don't have nappies to change but I could help Fitilwyn collect the soggy moss from the edge of the marsh and dry it by the fire. Dry moss was ideal for cleaning a baby's bum and could also be used as a sort of nappy.

Beorn was only a month or two old when Fitilwyn could see by his actions that he needed a pee or a poo and then hold him away from her while he did it. The rest of the time he was in close contact with her, strapped to her front in a pouch made of skins. He could reach her breasts from his pouch but sometimes she took him out and fed him more openly, cuddled in her arms. I loved watching.

When her sister's baby was born everyone was sure it was Gilamu come back to the world of men, as Zadolin had foretold. His spirit was just the same even though his body was different. They decided to call her Gilama. The Gods don't care whether you are a boy or a girl even if humans do.

Chapter 16 – Monkee Business

Almost every evening, after the Clan had finished their main meal of the day and before they went to bed wrapped in warm skins around the camp fire, there was an entertainment.

Sometimes it was a story told by one of the Clan. Often these were stories about the Gods and their spirit world, told by one of the old men who knew all the important traditions. Zadolin's story of the beginning of the World had been one of these. Other stories included a boring one by a much younger man telling about his recent hunts and how brave and successful he had been. Perhaps the best stories were pretty much like fairy tales but it wasn't just the kids who enjoyed them, it was everyone no matter how often they had heard them.

If it wasn't a story, it was music. Dancing was very popular and was mostly done to the rhythm of drums but some Clan members had made small flutes by drilling holes in the top of hollow bones. People danced on their own, getting more and more energetic as the rhythms went faster. No one had anything like beer or wine to drink, alcohol had obviously not been invented. None-the-less, the rhythm and the dancing often drove people into a state where they seemed to be drunk and sometimes had visions or said they did.

The singing was quite varied, sometimes like stories and more like a chant than a song, at other times they were proper songs with a tune you could dance to.

Everyone took a turn at doing an entertainment and would choose one they hoped they would be good at. They almost always chose a familiar story, song or dance because they knew people would like it and be able to join in even if their performance wasn't very good. But they wanted to be good because being good got you talked about and praised and admired. In our World people dream of singing or dancing on television and being famous and admired by the World. It was just the same here but your audience was about thirty members of the Clan not thirty million across the country. You felt just as good when you did a good show though.

When we could speak Clanguage pretty well and knew everybody (by name at last) they obviously thought it was time we joined the song and story rota. 'Can you do a song we haven't heard yet – one from your own country?' We said yes, then wondered what on earth we could do.

Our previous show business experience had been limited to one Children in Need concert at school in England. Each set of performers had to rehearse something, then get some sponsors to agree to pay up if the group got through its performance OK. With luck, other members of the audience would give more money if they thought your performance worth it.

Poppy and I had joined Dominic and Jacob as a group. Dominic played his guitar quite well, Jacob had two drums and some cymbals, Poppy was the main singer (she's good) and I tried to do some background singing but it was probably better when I didn't. We had a long debate about what we should sing and in the end it was Poppy who won the argument. 'Look, the people who come and listen will be all sorts of ages: Mums and Dads, grandparents, young brothers and sisters as well as our mates. We need a song everyone likes. Do you remember the dance in the market square? Everyone came and what everyone liked were the simple songs that you can dance to and which sounded like you had known them forever the first time you heard them. The best one that I remember well enough to sing is "I'm a believer".'

So we all practised being Monkees and changed the words a bit so it worked when a girl sang it. We were very happy with the result, people obviously liked the song and we got given quite a lot of money for the collection (but three other performers did better than us).

Poppy said 'Being Monkees worked last time, let's do it again.'

I wasn't so sure 'We haven't got a guitar or a drummer and my singing's even worse now my voice has broken.'

Poppy said it would be alright, we could ask one of the good drum players to help us and train a couple of the flute-players to play the tune. Then Poppy and I would do our best with singing the words.

We were worried about what language the words should be in, could we translate the English words into something that would make sense in Clanguage?' We decided to leave it in English. 'They wanted a song from our country, so they shouldn't mind a language they can't understand. Anyway, the words aren't really important even in England, it's the tune and the rhythm that matters.'

Poppy had been right, everyone loved the song and made us sing it many times before they were all tired with dancing to it.

Afterwards we knew what it must be like to be famous, everyone stopped to ask if we would we teach the song to their child or did we want to be de-loused? Poppy even got asked to join four boys on a hunt. Girls never went hunting.

Poppy's hunt was a fairly safe and easy one, the boys had obviously decided to take care of their new friend and a girl in the hunting party was a totally new experience for them.

The four boys called the fastest running dogs to come with them and they set off with quite small spears and spear-throwers. It was autumn but there wasn't much snow yet. Despite that, some of the mountain hares had started to go white and were easy to see. The hunt consisted of creeping up on a hare until you were near enough to release the dogs. The dogs would chase the hare madly and either catch it themselves or the hare would run too close to a hunter and get speared.

The hares were delicious and everyone praised Poppy's unique skill as a female hunter even though she hadn't actually caught a hare herself. She said next time they should go for a bison but didn't seem very upset when the boys decided to go back to all male hunting parties.

Because of her skill at singing, Poppy had been asked to join a hunt before I was. It made me very jealous.

Hunting the bigger animals can be dangerous and requires a lot of skill and co-ordination between the members of the hunting party. That's why it took so long before anyone decided to risk letting me join a hunt. The first time there were four top-class hunters and me. My job was to carry the spare spears and spear-throwers and help bring the dead animals home. The real hunting was left to the experts.

I slowly got to know what I was doing and was eventually allowed to be one of the proper hunters. It was a real triumph when the dogs chased a decent-sized wild boar straight towards me and I managed to get my spear firmly into its side, while a dog risked biting at the boar's neck. The boar was squealing in agony. I remembered the English phrase "squealing like a stuck pig" and I felt I ought to be ashamed of killing the poor pig and in such an inhumane way. But I wasn't. I had really enjoyed the thrill of the chase and of being able to bring home a meal for the Clan. I'd always hated blood-sports at home and those who killed animals for fun. This was different, the Clan were using the best hunting kit they had invented and a speared pig probably suffered less than one being torn apart by a pack of wolves. Anyway, the Clan needed meat to eat – but I had to admit that hunting was great fun too.

I usually went hunting with the same group of four boys and young men and half a dozen dogs. Everyone except me knew about the seasonal movements of the herd animals (bison, horses and reindeer mainly) and where to find the smaller prey at anytime of year. Sometimes the hunt would take us two or three days march from home and we would make camp for the night. It was usually pretty cold and everyone cuddled up close to each other and often enjoyed some mutual de-lousing. Being such close friends like this welded the group together and helped us know exactly what everyone would do in the hunt. I think if someone from our time had joined the group he would have said 'They must all be gay' but it wasn't like that at all. Everyone had girlfriends, and maybe kids, waiting for them on their return from the hunt.

It wasn't only bison, pigs and deer we hunted. Fishing provided fairly easily caught excellent food. The usual fishing tool was in the shape of a spear but with a vicious three-barbed piece of carved reindeer antler attached to the end. Ours were exactly the same as the ones I'd seen in the museums at home.

Usually it was trout, or some other fish about the same size, that we speared but in the autumn things had got much more exciting. This was the time of the salmon run when huge numbers of salmon swam up the river from the sea on their way of the streams at the head of the river, where they would mate and lay their eggs. There were so many salmon, and they were mostly concentrating on getting past natural obstacles like waterfalls, that it is absurdly easy to catch as many as you want. The spare ones could be smoked back at the cave fire and lasted quite a long time after the salmon run had finished.

I described all this to Poppy while she was helping prepare some salmon for smoking.

'Oh I know all about salmon runs – I bet you had loads of bears catching the fish, as well as you.'

'How on Earth did you know that?'

'Because I've seen it at least three times on television. The rivers in Canada are still full of salmon and when the bears turn up and start fishing it makes a really good nature programme.'

I told Poppy that ours were brown bears, the same sort that still live in parts of Europe. They seemed to be quite happy to let us join them fishing as long as we kept a decent distance away from them. Sometimes people found the skeletons of giant cave bears but no one had ever seen a living one.

Poppy and I had been really surprised to find hunting dogs living with the Clan – they must be quite an advanced people if they knew how to domesticate animals, although dogs were the only animals they had. Their dogs looked a bit like Alsatians but woollier.

The dogs spent a lot of time playing with the children or begging for food. It was the puppies that were the real surprise, quite often a woman with a baby would pick up a puppy and let it suckle from her breast. When we could speak the language well enough, Poppy asked one of the girls she de-loused why mothers fed puppies.

'It helps to make them tame and friendly with the children but that's not the main reason. If you are producing more milk than your baby wants to drink it hurts and if all your milk is not being drunk you might not produce enough when your baby is bigger and more hungry. So the puppies help get rid of the surplus milk. But maybe the most important thing is that the longer your milk is being drunk, by baby or puppy or both, the longer you'll wait before your moon-bleeds start again and you are likely get pregnant. Most mothers don't want another baby before the first one is big enough to feed itself properly.'

So puppies were Stone Age contraceptives. I'd never read that in a book.

What is in all the books is that dogs were domesticated for hunting and the Niaux dogs were very good at it. When I had become part of a hunting party I saw how it usually worked. Half the hunters hid in bushes, usually in a narrow trackway or path between two rocky outcrops. The others, and all the dogs, circled round and tried to drive a deer or wild boar towards the hiding hunters. It worked a treat and, because there were lots of deer and boar and not many people, it really didn't take that long to kill enough for everyone for several days. Hunting for food was certainly not a full time job.

I asked the hunters about the dogs, there seemed to be loads of puppies and yet there were only about twelve adult dogs. Did they let some go back to the wild or eat them? They seemed quite horrified at the idea of eating dogs and explained that they waited until the middle of winter, when the dogs had lovely, thick, warm fur and decided which were the friendliest and the best hunters. They took the rest off, well away from the camp, and knocked them on the head. They made superb skins. They told the children the skins were wolves and that the dogs had run away when they saw the wolves. The children were very fond of the dogs but everyone was grateful for the wolf skins, even the mothers who had suckled them.

Chapter 17 – The Cave Party

Evenings after dinner were story time most often. Poppy and I had done our turn at singing but now we could speak Clanguage properly I was asked to take my turn at telling a story.

It took me a long time to think about it. Could I just modify a story from home? It didn't seem to work. Eventually I decided on a story which had some sort of moral and would be set in the world familiar to the Clan. Here it is:

Most of the herds of bison and horses had moved away and so four hunters and their dogs had been gone for two days, far from home, hoping to find some wild boar. The dogs had disappeared barking furiously, which was a good sign. The hunters followed the dogs and found they had cornered a big sow who had three piglets with her. The sow could have killed a dog easily, so the dogs kept their distance while the hunters got closer and made two good shots with their spear-throwers. The sow was terribly wounded but not yet dead so the hunters expected her to squeal and bleed and die. Instead she started talking to them

'Soon I want you to kill me, the pain is terrible and I want to get to the spirit world. But first I want you to make me a promise, if you keep it you will become famous.'

'What is it you wish, O pig?'

'You must take my three babies and keep them like you keep your dogs. They will grow big and friendly and you will find them useful.'

'We will obey O pig, now we must kill you, let us approach and do it quickly.'

When it was done one of the hunters said 'A talking pig, it must have been a God living inside a pig, we must be careful to do what we promised'.

The piglets stayed near the body of their dead mother and were easy to catch. Two hunters put the dead sow on a pole and carried it home while the other two carried the little piglets.

Back home everyone was pleased to have some excellent pork to eat and were not too surprised about the tale of the piglets, it was just the sort of thing Gods do to humans when they feel like a bit of fun. The piglets were tiny and could only drink milk. The girls with babies often fed puppies and putting a piglet to the breast did not seem that different. As the pigs grew they switched to eating any waste food around the campfire and what they could find in the woods but they stayed as friendly to humans as if they had been breast-fed puppies.

There were two sows and a boar. When they reached adulthood the sows started to have babies of their own. The pigs became a nuisance, there were too many of them and they started stealing food and digging up useful plants. So the pigs ended-up living inside fenced enclosures and the people had to collect food for them. At least the pigs started to be useful because it was decided that the Gods would allow people to eat those that had been born in captivity.

By the time the children who had seen the first piglets be born, were grown and with children of their own, *there were pig pens all round the camp. Feeding all the pigs used up a lot of everyone's time.*

Twenty summers on and there were even more pig pens. The really important people in the Clan decided the pigs and the pens were theirs and that the less important people must spend nearly all of their time finding food for pigs.

Eventually the people forgot what it was like to be hunters, to know the habits of all the different animals, and how to catch salmon or find the best plants to eat. They no longer had time to spend ages each day listening to stories, dancing, singing and looking for lice. They seemed not to mind but if they had not forgotten the old life they would have minded.

As for the pigs, they thought it was great to spend all day snuffling in their pens and waiting for nice food to be brought to them.

They tried to be philosophical about being butchered eventually but knew it would be a safe way to the spirit world. There were lots more tame pigs than there had ever been when they were wild boar. They thought that taming humans to work for them had been a really good idea.

Had they been able to remember what it was like to search for food and mates in the wild woods and face the risk of death by humans or wolves but to know that you had a good chance of getting away or winning the fight, they might have changed their minds too.

Everyone seemed to enjoy the story but it didn't do what I wanted. The story was meant to be a warning about how domesticating animals would change human life for ever and not for the better either. I don't think anyone in the Clan got the message but even if they had, so what? I knew what they didn't – that, some generations in the future, humans were going to domesticate (or be domesticated by) a few of the World's species of animals and plants. Humans would then be almost enslaved, spending their lives looking after the farmed plants and animals that had become the most successful organisms on Earth.

I knew this was going to happen because, of course, it already had, thousands of years in the past from our World. There was nothing the Clan could do to change history even if, from their point of view, it wasn't history – it was the future.

On all the hunting parties, stories would be told about famous hunts of the past and how one could get really difficult prey. One of the best stories was about hunting reindeer and killing a whole lot all at once. I'd never seen it done and neither had any of the other hunters. One day we had a chance to see if it worked.

Some reindeer had moved into a rather narrow, steep-sided valley with a river running down it. At the end of the valley the river tumbled down a cliff as a waterfall. We skirted round and got ourselves and the dogs in at the top of the valley and then moved along the river-bank quite openly so the reindeer saw us and ran further down the valley towards the waterfall. When they got near the end of the valley we let all the dogs go and ran screaming at the deer ourselves. Most of them dashed towards the waterfall and fell over the cliff. There were seven dead deer waiting for us at the foot of the cliff and it took a lot of effort to get them all home.

That evening, when everyone had finished congratulating us on such a successful hunt, talk turned to what we should do with all the deer. It was Zadolin who came up with a really good idea.

'There's much too much meat for us to use before it goes bad. We should have a big party and ask everyone from the clans within a couple of day's march whether they would like to come. It'll be fun and might bring some boys and girls from other clans to come and join us. Our clan needs to be a bit bigger.'

He added 'We also need to thank the Gods for giving us all the food we need. Part of the celebrations will be in the secret chamber deep in the cave on the side of the valley where all the paintings of the animal Gods are. We can feast and dance to thank the Gods for all their help.'

Groups of men were sent off to visit all the nearby clans and invite them to come. Almost all said 'Yes' but most would send mainly their young men and girls who didn't yet have babies. These were the people who most wanted to come – it was like an online dating-site for them. The elders didn't often want a long walk and those with babies needed to care for them and help keep their own clan going.

News from the clan the furthest away to the north was worrying. They were too scared to risk coming because a cannibal tribe from even further north had invaded their lands and had captured, killed and eaten two of their children. Everyone in their clan was needed to defend it and try to exterminate the cannibals.

One evening Poppy told me 'I think this party will be on my birthday.' I asked how she knew. 'My moon-bleeds of course. My first here was two weeks after we arrved, then every four weeks until number twelve that has just finished. That means that, in another two weeks, we shall have been here a year – the day of the party."

In the end seven clans sent about thirty people to join our clan of nearly the same number. Of course the visitors were almost all young adults but our Clan included everyone from the newest babies to the oldest wise men and women.

Our tribe had just had two happy events: the birth of Beorn to Fitilwyn and me and the birth of Gilama to Fitilwyn's sister and Fermin. Zadolin decreed that part of the festivities would be a kind of christening to thank the Gods for giving the Clan some much needed new blood.

The seven reindeer were roasted slowly over the Clan's main fire. It took several days and then the cooked venison was carried down to the secret Niaux chamber where it would be re-heated and eaten. The hot sauce for the meal was a secret concoction whose recipe was known only to two of the elders. It was a kind of soup with lots of different vegetables and a whole variety of mushrooms, some of which looked worryingly like poison toadstools.

The soup was carried down to the chamber in big leather water bags and then poured into a natural depression in the rock. There had been a huge puddle in the depression but that had been emptied out and replaced with cold soup. Finally a fire was lit in the chamber that supplemented the light provided by several fat-based torches burning on the walls.

The fire heated large stones that were then dropped in the soup. Eventually the soup was hot and the reindeer meat pulled off the bone and added to the soup. The feast was ready and almost sixty of us filled the secret chamber and looked at the mysterious paintings while eating our fill.

After the meal the paintings seem to start changing. The torches flickered and made the animals seem to come alive. Zadolin started chanting and entreating the animal Gods to protect the Clan – perhaps he was thinking about cannibals. Lots of people started dancing energetically to drum-beats, working themselves into a frenzy before collapsing exhausted.

Poppy and I were feeling very odd but very happy. We felt we were one with the Clan and the animal Gods, we were part of nature and what we wanted to do most of all was to make love to each other.

Looking round, quite a lot of the other couples were acting on similar thoughts.

Poppy said 'Oh Moth, I think we are going to be part of the Clan for ever and that won't be too bad will it? We've been here about a year now, and I'm sixteen topday. Maybe we can risk having a baby and being a full part of the Clan?'

I didn't take much persuading and we were soon cuddled up together near the fire, while the animal Gods watched us and still danced on their wall. It was the first time for Poppy but it wasn't at all like my first time with Fitilwyn. Poppy took a much more active part in our love-making and seemed to know exactly what to do. When it was over we simply curled round each other, stroking and cuddling. Then our private reverie was interrupted by a small child's voice.

'Can I wriggle into bed with you?'

It was Albarran of course. Had he been waiting and watching until our love-making was over? Well, if he had been he would have seen much the same thing whichever couple he looked at!

We let him join us once Poppy had told him to go and have a wee first and he had done so. He wriggled right in between us making more post-love-making cuddles impossible.

Poppy smiled and said 'Well, we'd decided to have a baby hadn't we?'

'That should have taken nine months though' I pointed out.

Chapter 18 – Lost and Found

When we woke it took a moment to remember where we were and when we did it was scary. It was also completely dark, not just like a dark night but a complete absence of light and hence of vision. The torches must have burnt out ages ago and the fire gone out. All the rest of the Clan must have left, even little Albarran who had been curled up asleep with us. So we were alone in a dark cave, a kilometre underground and no real idea of how to find the way out. We had a rough idea which direction the exit must be and we might be able to feel our way along the walls of the cave but if we went wrong we'd be really lost.

Our best bet seemed to be to wait until some of the Clan came back with their torches and rescued us. We were certain our friends in the Clan would search for us as soon as they noticed we'd got lost. After a very long wait (we had no way of guessing how long) we saw a glimmer of light and heard some voices. As they got nearer we realised it wasn't the Clan, they were speaking the wrong language. Poppy whispered 'Did you teach them French?' 'No.' It was soon obvious that these French speakers were a tourist group with a guide and electric torches, come to see the prehistoric paintings. We stayed quiet, wondering what to do, until two of the visitors spotted us. 'Look at them! What a good idea to have a couple of people dressed up as cavemen. It helps you to imagine what it was like when they painted the bison.' 'And what they smelt like' said her companion. The guide heard the chatter and spotted us. 'Who are you and what are you doing here?' I replied quickly, in case Poppy gave away the real story. 'We explored a little cave and got completely lost. We dropped our torch and couldn't find our way out. Please can you lead us out? I think our parents might be getting worried.'

One of the tourists said 'I heard at the centre that some people were looking for a couple of lost kids' so the guide decided to lead us out straight away.

He said 'I'm afraid the whole group will have to come with me. I'll bring you back as soon as I can and you'll get your money back.'

'Don't worry about that' they said 'we're pleased to have helped find them. I wonder why they are dressed as cavemen?'

We didn't try to explain and they didn't ask us. We were so pleased that they just wanted to get us back to our parents who probably wouldn't mind what we smelt like.

At the centre booking office was a noticeboard which had a couple of photos of us, looking like ordinary children, and Mum's mobile number to phone if we were spotted. Mum and Dad were there in ten minutes, thanking everyone in sight and then whisking us off in the car.

'Why didn't you phone us when you were lost?'

'We left our phones in the cave where we camped and got lost without them. We lost track of time a bit, how long have we been away?'

'It was only one night after the night we left you but we were worried sick trying to find you. How did you get so appallingly dirty and smelly in two nights?'

'It seemed longer' was the only reply I could think of. Not much good, but they didn't quiz us for details – they just got us home and told us each to have a good bath, me first because Poppy wasn't quite as filthy as I was.

There was just time to get a private whisper to Poppy.

'Get your necklace and my baby-gift wrapped up and hidden in the old toy box. Our clothes can go in black rubbish sacks and we'll deal with them outside tomorrow. Oh, and can you cut your hair a bit and help me do mine when I have had my bath? I don't think Mum and Dad have noticed how long our hair has got in what they think is just a couple of days.'

I managed to find the bottle of louse-shampoo that had been in the medicine cupboard, slowly going out of date, since I was nine. It was a really good bath and the shampoo still seemed to work. I left nearly half of it for Poppy.

It ought to have been nice to be back, each in our own bed, in our own rooms. But we were both worried about the Clans-folk who had been our family and friends for so long. Fitilwyn and Beorn were there. Had there been an attack on the Clan to cause them to abandon us? Or had they simply woken up and found us gone? Would Fitilwyn be grieving for me? And my baby son?

Then I thought 'Even if he lived a long and happy life he would have died twelve thousand or so years ago, along with all the Clan.' A lonely thought.

And Poppy? I wanted Poppy. For a year we had spent our nights wrapped up together in warm skins by the Clan fire. Separate rooms in single beds with clean bedclothes wasn't quite the same.

We were both up early next morning and said we wanted to go and say hello to all the animals.

First we cleaned our cave clothes as well as we could and hung them in a barn to dry and lose some of their smell. We were pretty certain that Mum and Dad would think they were just the clothes we had made ourselves and not notice how much better made these were.

Our biggest priority was to decide what to tell Mum and Dad about our adventures. 'We can't tell them the truth, no one would ever believe us and they would probably wonder if we were going mad.' In the end it seemed best to stick with what we had already said: we had gone exploring in a cave, got lost and been rescued after a day or so. They seemed to believe us and didn't ask awkward questions like wanting to see, when we went to get our phones back, what the cave that had led us into the important Niaux caves looked like. The Niaux cave system is supposed to be all locked-up and protected so they might well have wondered about how we had got in.

There were a few awkward moments: for example quite a lot of our clothes seemed a bit too small for us.

Mum asked 'What's happened to you, anyone would think you were lost for a year not about a day!'

We had forgotten that we were really over sixteen now, not a day or two after Poppy turning fifteen as Mum and Dad thought. All we could do was to mutter about lots of our friends having had a spurt of growth before the holidays. Perhaps it was our turn now?

Then there was the Mountain Avens incident. Mountain Avens doesn't grow near our house in France, only at much higher altitude. One day we had driven up to the ski-station (closed for the summer) and found the plant in bloom. Mum asked if we knew what the flowers were.

Without thinking we both said 'Anderlores.'

'Where on earth did you get that name? What language is it?'

Poppy and I looked at each other and she realised quicker than me what she needed to say. 'A lady we met near Niaux showed us one of these flowers. Her name for it must have been some local dialect word.'

It's marvellous what you can get away with when you tell the truth, as long as you don't tell all the truth. We'd learnt this name, like we'd learned the names of hundreds of plants and creatures, from the Clan. Even the children knew the names of every plant and animal they found and whether they were good to eat, or could go to Zurine to be made into medicine or were best left alone. We already knew the names of some of the plants in English or French but when we learned a new one from the Clan we had just started using the Clanguage name even if we were talking to each other in English or French. We'd need to be careful not to fall into that trap again.

Phillippe and Emilie were back home from a visit to friends in Spain and we had another few weeks to play with them before school started again.

I think Mum and Dad were relieved to see us resume our old ways, playing with friends, helping Étienne with his cows and begging to go to the market each Saturday. But whenever we could we disappeared to the Juniper Rock, just the two of us, to talk about our life in the Stone Age.

The first question we asked ourselves was 'Did it all really happen?' If it didn't, it was all some sort of dream but a dream we both had and during which we seem to have got over a year older even though the dream lasted a couple of days or less. What's more, you don't usually bring stuff home with you from a dream. It must have been real and we just wished we knew how to make time-travel work, so we could go back and see the Clan again one day.

We knew the stuff we brought back was really important, no one's ever seen real Stone Age clothes and no one even seems to have guessed that they made gold jewellery like Poppy's necklace. My baby-gift from Fitilwyn wasn't so unusual, there seem to be quite a lot like it in the museums and on their websites.

We sprayed the clothes with some stuff that was supposed to kill cockroaches and all other insects. We thought that would solve the louse problem and then we dried the clothes out, rolled them up in plastic sacks and stored them away. When they asked, we told Mum and Dad we had put them in one of the barns because they were so filthy.

'Poppy, there's one other thing we brought back that we haven't thought about. It might be the most important thing of all.'

'What's that Moth?'

'Clanguage: no one except us knows anything about the language that was spoken by cavemen. We can speak it quite well and we mustn't forget it and lose it.'

We decided to finish writing the book that we had started before we became cavemen but instead of writing it down we talked for ages to each other, in Clanguage, about everything that had happened to us and recorded it all on our tablets.

'Now we won't forget the language or what happened and when we are ready to finish our book all we have to do is listen to our story and write it down in English.'

We'd just started back at school. We had taken our Brevet exams at the end of last term – they're a bit like GCSE but a year earlier. We both got good marks so now we were moving up to the Lycée and starting to study for our BAC (university entrance) exams. We had said last term which BAC course we wanted to do. English people think the BAC is like A-levels but it's not. It takes three years, not two, and you do lots of different subjects, not just three or four, but you can choose the area you want to specialise in. Before the summer I'd said I wanted to take sciences (so I could study biology at university) but now I had changed my mind and asked to take the history and language course instead.

Poppy asked 'Aren't you interested in moths any more?'

I replied 'Yes, but I want to learn how to understand languages properly, so I can see how Clanguage works and which of today's languages it might have evolved into. That way I might really discover something new, it's still a sort of science. I'll always be interested in moths but I think getting a job to study them would be really difficult, they'll just be a hobby.'

Poppy had changed her mind too. 'I was going to do history and languages too but I've decided to do sciences. I really want to be an archaeologist who studies the cave cultures; it's the only way I shall ever get a really good look at all the caves round here that the public aren't allowed in. The university websites say sciences are more important than history for archaeology. So now we've swapped choices!'

Chapter 19 – A Happy Event

We had both been doing, and enjoying, our BAC studies for a couple of weeks when Poppy asked if we could go up to the Juniper Rock – she had something to tell me.

'I've got something for you Moth' and handed me a little parcel.

Inside was a carved image of a girl, you could see her face and braided hair, not like the baby-gift carvings the Clan made.

'This looks a bit like a Clan carving – do you know who made it?'

'Fitilwyn showed me one just like this. Her father had given it to her, he had brought it back from his travels when he had met her mother and brought her and her brother home to the Clan. Fitilwyn said you wanted one with a face on it, not like the one she made you.'

'Is that your face? It looks more like hers.'

'It's neither, I never got round to trying to carve one myself. This is a copy of a famous Venus figurine, one of the few with a proper face. I bought it off the internet I'm afraid.'

I was really pleased with it and asked Poppy 'Why are you giving it to me now? It's ages to Christmas!'

'It wasn't the time before – at least I wasn't sure it was. It's a baby-gift.'

'You're going to have a baby? Are you really sure?'

'Yes and yes. You know how things work, I haven't had a "moon-bleed" since we were rescued from the cave.'

'So it was just that once, the cave party with Albarran getting in the way between us?'

'He obviously didn't get in the way enough did he?'

'Poppy, I love you, you know that don't you? I'd always thought we'd have babies one day. One day, but not quite yet. How are we going to tell Mum and Dad?'

'I'm not looking forward to it at all. Will you help? I don't think I dare tell them on my own.' 'Of course I will. Perhaps they'll like the idea of being grandparents while they are still fairly young.'

They didn't. They were furious and worried and disappointed in us all at once.

'We warned you and you absolutely promised you'd be careful to avoid babies before university.'

I said 'We were lost and scared in the cave. We really meant to be careful but we just cuddled up together once. That sort of accident happens sometimes doesn't it?'

Perhaps Mum and Dad remembered their first visit to watch the marmots or Poppy's Mum's party. Anyway, they calmed down and were really nice to us again. After asking Poppy how she was feeling and how long ago it had all happened (we said during Poppy's birthday treat when we were lost in the cave). Mum said 'Well at least it's not been too long, we'll go and see the doctor tomorrow.'

'What do you mean?' asked Poppy.

'When very young girls get pregnant by mistake the doctor can give them some pills to make the pregnancy end. You'll be back to normal and back at school in no time.'

I looked at Poppy and could see what she was thinking before she started to say it.

'I don't want you to poison my baby. I was an unexpected baby after Mummy's party. If she had decided to have me killed before I was born I'd never have known about it but I would have missed my whole life. I've enjoyed nearly everything that's happened to me and I think Moth has too, so I'm really glad you didn't have him poisoned either. He was an accidental baby, like me, I think. I want my baby to have its life too.'

'And so do I – I was an accident wasn't I Dad?'

He didn't say anything but nodded slightly. I think Poppy had made both of them get close to crying. They never mentioned abortions again and we all started planning for May when they would become grandparents. I think they were almost looking forward to it after all.

Mum took Poppy to see the special teacher at school who helps sort things out for children who had problems at home or were failing to cope with life.

She talked mainly to Mum 'It's happened before and we can cope easily enough. Poppy can stay at school until a month or six weeks before the birth.

Then perhaps she'll want to stay at home with her baby until the end of the summer holidays, she's very clever so she'll soon catch-up on her studies. If you and your husband can look after the baby on school days, Poppy can come back to school in September and carry on with studying until she's got her BAC.'

She also added 'Unlike England, it's not illegal for a boy to have sex with a girl as long as she says "yes" and is over fifteen. It sounds as though Timothy and Poppy stayed one day the right side of the law. If they'd still been in England, where the age is sixteen I think, they might have been in trouble.'

When Poppy told me this she said 'Don't worry, I was really sixteen – it was my birthday in the Stone Age even if people think I'm only fifteen now. Of course Fitilwyn was only about twelve but I don't think they worried about the age of consent in those days.'

Poppy went to the expectant mothers' clinic every month or so to be checked and scanned.

After one visit she called me into her room and said 'She's a girl, what would you like to call her? I want you to choose.'

I didn't know what to say. I kept thinking of Fitilwyn, it's a lovely name but I thought Poppy might not like our baby to be named after the mother of my first baby. Also it would be ever so difficult to explain to everyone where the name had come from. Suddenly, still thinking about Fitilwyn, I remembered what her name had meant and said:

'Shall we have a flower name like yours Poppy? What about Anemone? They'll still be out in May when she's born.'

'I think that's a lovely name Moth; I'm glad I let you choose and I was a bit afraid you might choose Fitilwyn.'

'Well, you did get a baby gift that looks like her – do you want me to change my mind?'

'No, I don't, Anemone's got a name now.'

When May came I could see Poppy was getting worried and I wasn't surprised. I hadn't asked her about the details and I had never really understood how a full-sized baby could get out the way it had got in. It must be really painful. Then I realised she was more likely to be worrying about something much more serious: what had happened to her Mum. Was there anything I could say that might reassure her? I couldn't think of anything and was just as worried myself as she must be. In the end it was Poppy who got us talking about it.

She asked 'Do you worry about having a car crash when we drive back to England?'

'No of course not, Mum and Dad are safe drivers.'

'What about when we fly?'

'It's OK but I do wonder when the wings are going to fall off and feel a bit scared sometimes.'

'Yes, I think most people are like that but it's not logical. Driving in a car is quite dangerous, people are killed on the roads every day in France. Ryanair have never killed anyone yet and they've flown millions of people. I know what happened to Mummy is ever so rare, probably rarer than air crashes and very much rarer than car crashes. I know I don't need to worry but I still do.'

'Would you like me to come with you when you go to have Anemone?' 'I wish I knew. I think I might like you there, to hold my hand. But then I think I'd be worrying about you worrying, when I should be thinking about what the nurses tell me to do and then looking after the baby when she comes. I think I'll ask the nurse at the clinic what she thinks.'

After her next visit, Poppy said I could come if I really wanted to but the nurse said it was often easier if the boy didn't come when he and the mother were quite young. I remembered what Fitilwyn had said when Beorn was due and was secretly quite relieved.

So when I first met Anemone she was with Poppy cuddled up in bed having a drink of milk. Poppy smiled at me and said 'They are air-bags now aren't they? Much too big.'

'Of course they aren't, that's what they're for and they look lovely. So does she. How will you feed her when you go back to school?'

'I've got to use a little milking machine so I can leave milk in bottles for Mum to feed her while I'm at school.'

'Étienne says milking by hand is better than a machine, shall I ask him to teach me how to do it?' Smiling, she said 'I'm not one of his cows – I'll use the machine thank you.'

Poppy was back home only two days after Anemone was born. She would have almost four months at home before she started school again in September. I, on the other hand, had a couple more months of school before the summer holiday started.

I asked Mum and Dad if I could share a room with Poppy and Anemone. They seemed a bit uncertain:

'Does she want you, as well as the baby, to keep her awake?'

Poppy claimed that she did want me with her 'I'll teach him to change nappies and cuddle Anemone if she is still crying after she has had a feed.'

Mum wanted a chat with Poppy before making a final decision and Poppy told me all about it when next we visited the Juniper Rock. Mum didn't want any more accidental babies (and neither did Poppy nor I for that matter). Mum was realistic enough to know that she couldn't really trust us not to take risks, whether we shared a bed or simply went off on walks alone together. So Mum told Poppy that, if she wanted, she could get a prescription for contraceptive pills suitable for young mothers (pills that wouldn't reduce the amount of breast-milk she made). Poppy had agreed to the pills and promised to take them regularly once the doctor said it was time to start. Meanwhile, while Anemone was very young, we both had to promise to be good. Poppy said 'I don't think I'd want to yet anyway.'

So the bunk-beds were taken down and fixed at ground level as a nice big double-bed with the cot on Poppy's side. As I lay there, beside Poppy, I realised that this was only the second time we'd shared a proper double bed, the Pic du Midi had been almost four years ago. It seemed much longer and had been, given that we'd lived that extra year with the Clan.

You can probably imagine the sort of comments that I got when the news spread at school about Poppy and Anemone. Some of the boys were crude 'Don't you know how to use capotes anglaises? You should. You're English.' But most seemed interested and not sure if they were jealous of me or not.

The girls were quite different, they wanted to know every little detail of how we were rearing Anemone, how we had chosen her name, and whether we were still sleeping together (answer: yes but a young baby generally means all you want to do is sleep and anyway childbirth doesn't leave a new mother very interested in sex-play). When the boys realised how much attention I was getting from the girls they stopped their snide comments and took an interest in my new role in life. They wanted to show how interested in babies they were and what great dads they would make given half a chance.

At last it was the summer holidays. We had a little baby-sling so Poppy or I could carry Anemone close on our chest. It was almost exactly the same way everyone in the Clan had carried their babies. We enjoyed taking gentle walks around the village and along the road to the shower-bath but what we liked best, in good weather, was climbing the Juniper Rock and setting up a picnic camp there. Lying on her rug, Anemone didn't need to wear much except sun-cream.

We lay there in the sun too, taking turns to feel our fingers gripped so strongly by Anemone. I just loved watching as Poppy took off her T-shirt to offer Anemone her feed and I remembered a question I'd meant to ask one of the mothers in the Clan but had never summoned up the courage.

'Poppy, what does it feel like to feed a baby? I remember kiss-feeding kids and really feeling good about it. Is it like that? Or is it like when you let me pretend to be a baby?'

'Both really. Sometimes my nipples get sore and it hurts when she feeds but I still know inside that I want to feed her and being the only way she can get her food feels pretty much the way I felt when I kiss-fed a kid. But usually it's much better than that, it makes me feel a bit sexy, just like when you suckled me, and makes me fall in love with our baby. Also, when she was really new, it seemed to help all my insides get back to the proper place and shrink down to their proper size.'

'Do you remember the Clan mothers mostly let puppies take milk from their breasts? Do you want a puppy?'

'No!'

'Not even if I'm the puppy?'

'Oh, I suppose Anemone won't mind if you are not too greedy. Let's see what it's like.'

Poppy's milk was warm, creamy and sweet, not at all like the cow or goat milk we usually bought from Étienne. I only needed to suck gently, her milk seemed almost to come by itself. I would have liked to drink lots but of course I didn't, it was time for Anemone's feed.

Poppy said she had enjoyed the experience as much as I had seemed to 'It made me feel quite sexy but I'm afraid that's all the sex I want until I have recovered a bit more from giving birth.'

'I wonder why the Clan mothers don't let their men do the puppies' work? We both enjoyed it, so I guess they would too.'

Poppy explained that she knew the answer to this question because she'd done a lot of Googling about milk while she was waiting for Anemone to arrive.

'Milk is actually poisonous to most grown-ups. Any milk, not just breast milk. At least three quarters of Chinese, Africans and Indians can't drink milk without getting severe indigestion, diarrhoea and farting like fury. It's called lactose intolerance because they don't have the enzyme that babies have to digest milk. It's only people like Europeans, who have had a good lot of milk from domestic animals for centuries, that have evolved to keep their baby enzymes as adults. Hardly any

Europeans have lactose intolerance but the Clan people had never had domestic milk-animals and so were almost certain to be completely lactose intolerant.'

'Poppy, can lactose intolerant people eat cheese?' 'Yes, as long as it's hard normal cheese. But the Clan people hadn't invented cheese.'

'No, but we have, Étienne makes lovely cow and goat cheese. I wonder what Poppy cheese would be like?'

'I hope that was a joke but you might like to know that American men with more money than sense (that's most of them) pay huge sums for human cheese. They are practically cannibals. That was on Google too.'

'So do you think I'm a cannibal or is milk OK but not cheese?' She ignored me.

When Anemone had finished her feed and been laid on some soft paper she could wee on if she wanted, we went back to a subject we had discussed here over two years ago.

'Do you remember talking about Aslan and whether there really was someone who "wrote the script" for our lives?'

'Yes, and we thought there probably wasn't, unless the script writer left plenty of gaps where we made our own choices, decisions and mistakes.'

'Well, I've been thinking about it some more and I'm totally confused. We spent a year with the Clan and that happened over 10,000 or 12,000 years ago.

Even if there isn't a script writer, once things have happened the script has written itself, you can't change what happened. So either we somehow imagined the whole story ourselves or the Clan was real and their story was written in the Stone Age. If their story was, then ours must have been too. So what we did then wasn't our choice, what was going to happen had already been decided.'

Poppy thought for a bit and then said 'One of the main reasons scientists say backwards time-travel is impossible is that a time-traveller could change things that had already happened and cause the whole of history to change. Suppose you had accidentally killed a Clan member who would otherwise have lived and been one of your 480 times great grandmothers. Would you just disappear? You should do.'

Poppy went on 'If the story is already written then impossible things like that can't happen. Everything feels like real life and you think you are making all your decisions but you are playing by the rules of a game that already exists. Just like playing a computer game, it's all down to your skill and decisions but someone else created the game and the rules.'

I thought for much longer than Poppy had. 'I think I've got my head round that, Poppy. But if your theory is right is it only the past that is fixed? Suppose someone came back from the future to visit us now. To them it would be the past and its story written. To us it is now and we have free will to write our own story.'

'Do we? How do you know? Provided you never know if the story is already written, or you are writing your own story, it will always seem like you are writing your own story. I can't think of any test that would let you to discover whether it was your story or one already created. So I think it makes sense to assume that we are making our own story and get on with enjoying our life and doing what we choose. Even if we are wrong we won't know, unless we find out after we die but I don't believe we will.'

I said 'Even people who believe in God seem certain they make their own decisions and write their own story. They say God decides what he wants people to do but then lets them choose for themselves whether to do what He wants. It must be very boring being all-powerful but then not making any decisions. Writing everyone's story would be much more fun. Still, if everyone agrees we should be responsible for our own actions, we'd better decide what we want to do with our lives.'

'You first Moth, what plans for your life?'

'You know the most important thing. It's you and Anemone. People think being stuck with a baby when you are only about sixteen is a terrible mistake That's not true: it's what was normal for thousands of years when humans first existed and when we lived with the Clan. I want you and two or three babies and a life together. No one else at school will do that for years yet. I'm really lucky.'

'Thank you Moth. I think we'll enjoy our life together whatever happens. I suppose we might get married one day but lots of young people in France don't. They live together and get a "certificate de concubinage" from the mayor. I think I'd be happy as your concubine.'

'Aren't men allowed to have more than one concubine in some countries? That might be interesting if we ever get back to the Clan! That's my big ambition, I want to find out how time-travel works and be able to use it to visit the Clan again, see our friends and especially Beorn. Do you mind about me and Fitilwyn and Beorn?'

'No, you asked my permission and I like Fitilwyn. I think we are sort of sisters and I'd love Beorn to meet his half-sister one day.'

'Thank you Poppy, I was worried about that but now I'm not. As for my work, of course I want to do well enough at university to get a really interesting job. You already know I hope that will be something to do with studying ancient languages.'

Poppy said 'My work ambition's no secret either, I want to be an archaeologist studying the Stone Age in particular. So it looks like we'll both need jobs at a university or a research centre.'

I replied 'I want to get back to the Clan, not just study Stone Age times at university. People will think I'm mad if I claim to have already done time-travel and fairly mad if sayI simply that I'm trying to find out if it's possible.

Finally, I've absolutely no idea how to start discovering how we made our visit to the Clan.'

Poppy agreed 'Yes, I want to go back to the Clan for a second visit and see all our friends again. If our first visit wasn't magic it must have been a result of something quite simple, there were no complex time-machines made by mad scientists. Both journeys happened overnight and it seems likely they were caused by something we did in the afternoon or evening of the day before. What did we do before the first journey? We played at being cavemen, used de-lousing to explore each other's bodies, ate a meal of wild boar, some nettles and those mushrooms Guillaume gave us. Do you remember after the meal? We both felt a bit odd, really contented with life and properly part of nature that was all round us. The homeward journey also started after we had similar feelings and after we had eaten the party food that the Clan had made, with a whole lot of wild mushrooms, mushrooms that made people seem intoxicated or drugged in some way.'

She concluded 'If we are going to look for how to do time-travel, I think we need to study magic mushrooms. The trouble is that is likely to be dangerous as well as illegal and getting the dosage right might be difficult, get it wrong and we might meet dinosaurs or get back home in the middle of the last war.'

I was amazed at how much thought Poppy had put into the time-travel question and I was almost certain she was right.

'I think we need to start by just getting to know all the kinds of mushrooms and toadstools that grow in this part of France and find out from books which ones are poisonous or hallucinogenic (I think that's the proper word for "magic"). We will need to photograph the ones we find and get help from experts with identifying them. It will be like when I was first interested in moths, fun as well as a scientific enquiry.'

A couple of weeks later I remembered it was August and Poppy would be sixteen the day-after tomorrow. Anemone had just gone to sleep in her cot and we were tucked up in bed. 'Poppy, what would you like to do for your birthday treat this year?'

'All my treats have been really exciting – our shower at Pic du Midi when I was twelve, talcum powder after the folk-dance when I was thirteen, Montsegur when I was fourteen and you learned about de-lousing, Niaux when I was fifteen where we tried de-lousing and ended up with the Clan, the first time I was sixteen and we were with the Clan at the Niaux party and you got me pregnant.'

Poppy went on 'According to the people in our World, I'll be sixteen again in a couple of days. We've got Anemone to think about so we should do something with her. Let's walk up to the Top of the World carrying Anemone in her sling, we can share doing that with Mum and Dad. They might drive up with a picnic for all of us if we ask nicely.'

'That sounds a great idea but it certainly won't be as much fun as your other birthdays. The penalty of being parents I suppose.'

'Never mind, you can give me an early present if you like.'

'I haven't got one yet, I was going to the market tomorrow.'

'I don't think you need to wait. It's three months since Anemone was born, I'm quite recovered and I've started taking those pills Mum got me. I'm almost sixteen but I don't think we need wait another two days because I was really sixteen last birthday. Anyway we're in France not England.' Poppy smiled at me. 'Can you remember what we did a year ago?'

I smiled back and found I hadn't forgotten a thing.

An Afterword from Poppy

I was about to be sixteen, for the second time, when our story ended. At least it felt like the end of the "really big adventure" that I had always wanted. Now I am a responsible Mum and a conscientious student. Not something that will make another good story.

Moth used the covid-virus outbreak to finish writing our story and we kept trying to improve it until we felt we would like to publish this book. That took ages. At last we had the courage to show our story to Mum and Dad who knew lots of it was true – they had been there, part of the events we described. But had we made up the visit to the Clan? Even they weren't quite certain but seemed to accept that we believed it to be true. We asked if we could publish it. 'Why not? We think it's an interesting story and no one is going to believe it's anything but a bit of fiction. They probably won't even believe that Moth wrote it.'

So now, at last, the book is ready to be published. Our lives have gone on and exciting things are still happening. I've found my real Dad. Both Moth and I hope to start university. My real Dad's a professor of astrophysics and interested in the possibility of time travel. If we ever do make a second visit to the Clan, I'll tell you all about it. It might be my turn as author this time, Moth's too busy learning the Basque language and trying to persuade me that Anemone needs a brother or sister.

Poppy Grove, Ariège, France